Ride or Die

Wanda Lauren Taylor

James Lorimer & Company Ltd., Publishers
Toronto

James Lorimer & Company Ltd., Publishers acknowledges the support of the Ontario Arts Council (OAC), an agency of the Government of Ontario, which in 2015–16 funded 1,676 individual artists and 1,125 organizations in 209 communities across Ontario for a total of $50.5 million. We acknowledge the support of the Canada Council for the Arts, which last year invested $153 million to bring the arts to Canadians throughout the country. This project has been made possible in part by the Government of Canada and with the support of the Ontario Media Development Corporation.

Cover design: Shabnam Safari
Cover image: iStock

Library and Archives Canada Cataloguing in Publication

Taylor, Wanda Lauren, author
　　　Ride or die / Wanda Lauren Taylor.

(SideStreets)
Issued in print and electronic formats.
ISBN 978-1-4594-1249-1 (softcover).--ISBN 978-1-4594-1250-7 (EPUB)

　　　I. Title.　II. Series: SideStreets

PS8639.A97R53 2017　　　　　jC813'.6　　　　　C2017-903308-5
　　　　　　　　　　　　　　　　　　　　　　　　　C2017-903309-3

Published by:
James Lorimer &
Company Ltd., Publishers
117 Peter Street, Suite 304
Toronto, ON, Canada
M5V 0M3
www.lorimer.ca

Distributed in Canada by:
Formac Lorimer Books
5502 Atlantic Street
Halifax, NS, Canada
B3H 1G4

Distributed in the US by:
Lerner Publisher Services
1251 Washington Ave. N.
Minneapolis, MN, USA
55401
www.lernerbooks.com

Manufactured by Friesens Corporation in Altona, Manitoba, Canada in July 2017.
Job #234942

*This book is dedicated to all those
who think they have a handle on
being normal;
and to all of those who know
that there is no such thing.*

Chapter 1

Friends Forever

"Kanika Grace Adams!" Kanika could hear Aunt Becky screaming from the kitchen window. But Kanika stayed outside and ignored the cries of the aunt who had raised her since she was five. Kanika was fifteen years old now. She wanted to be free of the tight grip Aunt Becky had on her. Kanika would go inside when she felt like it and not a minute before. She closed her eyes and stretched her arms wide. The wind pushed past her caramel face and swept her thick, dark curls into a frenzy.

"Go faster," she commanded her best friend Panama. Kanika was planted behind Panama on the bike seat.

"Okay!" Panama dug her heels deeper into the bike pedals. She pushed forward with all her might. Kanika squealed with excitement as the bike shot forward.

They came to a sudden stop at the top of Cooper's Hill. Kanika hopped off the back of the bike and ran through the thick grass. Panama dropped the bike and flew behind her. They got to the clearing and zipped past the park benches scattered under the maple trees. They plopped down on a freshly mowed patch of grass. Kanika stretched out on her back and stared at the sky. Panama followed.

"Let's just stay here forever," Kanika sang.

"But what would we eat?" Panama asked.

Kanika laughed.

The girls stared at the puffy, white clouds moving and separating across the sky.

"So, Kanika, who do you want to marry when you leave school?" Panama asked.

"Don't laugh. I think that Danny guy that comes around you-know-where is so sexy."

"Yeah, he is. Do you want to marry him?"

"I think so. Our children would be gorgeous little butterscotch babies."

"I might marry Gabe."

"Don't do it, Panama. He's creepy."

They laughed, then stared at the sky.

"Ever wonder what else is out there?" Panama broke the pleasant silence.

"Always," Kanika said. "As soon as we are old enough, let's leave Guysborough and find out."

"Okay!" Panama squealed excitedly.

Kanika closed her eyes and smiled.

"We have to go." Panama hopped to her feet, brushing the grass from her clothes. "My mom will be looking for me soon."

The girls were soon back on the bike, pushing the wind out of their path as they rode. Kanika wrapped her arms tightly around Panama's bony waist as they pedaled down Cooper's Hill at full speed. Kanika grinned. The warm country air breezed across her face and sent her hair flapping.

It wasn't long before the sun sank down behind the trees.

"It's getting late," Panama worried. "We should have been back a long time ago."

Kanika knew that Panama's mother was very strict. Sometimes Kanika could convince Panama to stay out a little longer than she was allowed. But this time, she sat back as Panama jolted and jerked along the dusty dirt road.

Aunt Becky was stern too, but Kanika often tested out what she could get away with. "Aunt Becky has probably called all around the neighbourhood looking for me by now."

"I wish I didn't care as much. Like you, Kanika."

"I just don't like all these rules. We're fifteen. Why do we still have to be inside before dark? Makes no sense."

"Well, I don't want to get grounded."

"You still get grounded?" Kanika laughed.

Panama was embarrassed. "Not anymore. I try not to make my parents mad."

The bike squeaked up the next hill and back down the other side toward home. Home was a tiny grove in Guysborough County, nestled in the eastern tip of Nova Scotia. Only four thousand people called it home, and the number went down every year. Kanika knew that young people left the country woods for life in the city of Halifax and beyond. She heard stories about college kids partying every weekend and tourists crowding the Halifax waterfront for summer events. She hoped to be able to leave Guysborough and see it for herself.

Guysborough had a large Black population. According to Aunt Becky, their family history in Guysborough went back six generations. Kanika and Panama met in school. Panama hadn't been born in Halifax. A Caucasian family had brought her over from China when she was nine months old. Since neither girl had any siblings, Panama was the closest thing Kanika had to a sister.

The bike came to a halt at the end of Kanika's driveway.

Kanika gave Panama a quick squeeze and hopped off. "See you at school tomorrow."

"Okay," Panama sang. Then she sped off toward home.

Aunt Becky swung the door wide open as Kanika skipped up the driveway.

"It's about time you got here, young lady," she said sternly. "I was about to send a rescue team out looking for you."

Kanika laughed. It was barely dark and Aunt Becky worried too much. Kanika slid past her aunt, who stood in the doorway with a hand on her hip.

"You have nothing to say?" Aunt Becky called after her.

"Nope." Kanika kept walking until she was down the hall and in her room. She closed the door and listened to see if Aunt Becky would come in behind her and yell. A few moments passed and the bedroom door stayed still. Kanika got undressed and climbed into bed.

"Peace," she whispered to herself. Then she slowly drifted off to sleep.

Chapter 2

The Hideout

The next day at school, Kanika and Panama were sitting side by side in Principal Tyner's office. There were only a few more weeks left before school closed for the summer. Panama was near tears.

"Why are you so scared, Panama?" asked Kanika.

"'Cause we're in big trouble, Kanika."

"No, we're not. We didn't do anything wrong."

"But we didn't report that fight between

Trevor and Andy. Now Mr. Tyner knows everything. He's going to call our parents."

The girls were the only two witnesses to the fight that morning between two guys on the basketball team. Andy had been beaten so badly he was taken to the hospital.

"What are you going to tell him?" Panama was scared.

"I'm gonna tell him I didn't see anything," Kanika responded.

"But that's a lie."

"Panama, how many times do I have to tell you? It's not cool to be a rat."

"Yeah, but I feel guilty lying."

"Because you're Asian?"

"What does that have to do with it?"

"Asian kids are super smart and super focused. They want to get perfect grades and please their parents."

"What movie were you watching? That's not true. Well, it's kind of true. But not for everyone." Panama pouted.

"Panama, do you remember what happened last time you tattled on someone?"

Kanika quietly reminded Panama of the time Maddie from their gym class had broken into Keisha's locker and stolen her makeup bag.

"Remember? You ran and told. And after school, Maddie and her friends beat the crap out of you. I'm not saying it was right that she stole. But sometimes getting involved just isn't worth the trouble."

Panama thought about it. "Okay, I'll lie," she agreed.

"Good."

Mr. Tyner stepped into the office. "Follow me, ladies."

Kanika and Panama followed Mr. Tyner around the back of the secretary's desk and into his office. He held his arm out to tell them to take a seat. Then he shut the door behind them. His stomach jiggled as he zipped behind the desk and fell into his chair.

"So, girls, do you know why I called you in to the office?"

"Well —" Panama started.

Mr. Tyner liked to talk and hardly listened. He went on before Panama had a chance to say another word. "I know you both saw that fight this morning. I need you to tell me what happened. Who started it?"

"Don't know." Kanika shrugged.

"Panama?"

Kanika could tell by the look on Panama's face. She was about to spill everything.

As Panama gave Mr. Tyner a play-by-play of the whole event, Kanika covered her face with her hands and shook her head. She couldn't believe that Panama told him every detail.

The two girls walked back to their classroom in silence.

Panama put her hand on the classroom doorknob and turned to Kanika. "Sorry," she said.

"Yeah, you're gonna be when Trevor finds out that you told on him. And I don't want any part of it."

Kanika pushed past Panama and swung the classroom door open. She quickly sat down and pulled out her binder. Panama walked in slowly with her head hanging. She clearly felt bad that she'd let down her friend.

Kanika was annoyed with Panama. But at the same time she felt bad about being angry. After class, she would let Panama know she wasn't mad at her.

Panama smiled with relief when Kanika let her know she wasn't mad. The two of them never stayed angry at each other for long. Not having a mother, Kanika always felt like a part of her was missing. Panama was without her real mother, too. Being friends gave them a sense of belonging. Especially when they felt like they didn't belong to the parents who had claimed them.

After school got out, the girls dropped

their bags and hopped on Panama's bike.
They were on the way to their secret hideout.
The bumpy dirt road soon veered off toward
a dead end. Panama squeezed the hand brake.
Kanika loosened her grip on Panama's waist
and the girls jumped off together. Panama
leaned the bike against a rusted guardrail.
It was the only thing separating the dirt road
from a thick forest of aspen and pine trees.
The girls squeezed past the "No Trespassing"
sign. They trudged through the pathways
covered in thick fern and grass.

Only Kanika, Panama and a few girls
from their street knew of the hideout. They
used to make their way there after school and
on weekends. Most times they talked boys,
sometimes school and always about which
famous person they would marry. But Panama
broke their code of secrecy when she began
inviting boys there. The boys started telling
others, and as school neared summer break,
word had started to spread. Now Kanika was

never sure who or what she would see when they arrived. She took in a deep breath, wondering what she would find this time.

The sun fell slightly to the west as the girls neared the swampy clearing. Panama's face lit up.

"I hope Gabe is there," she blurted out. Gabe was the boy who had been teaching Panama about older kid stuff, like kissing.

"Why would he be there?" asked Kanika. "Why did you tell *him* about this?"

"He wanted to know."

"But he's not even our age. The hideout is for kids our age. You shouldn't have told him."

"He's still a teenager, Kanika. Nineteen. It's the same thing."

Kanika sulked. She hated Gabe. She hated the way he laughed like he was the only one in on some stupid joke. She hated the wide space between his dark, round eyes. His nappy afro that looked like it hadn't seen a comb in weeks. The way he stared at people with a sly grin on his face.

"Don't be so selfish, Kanika. You don't own the hideout, you know."

The girls plodded through the path in silence, Kanika trailing behind Panama. When they reached the edge of the creek, Panama started to run. A reflection of the broken-down boathouse glistened over the warm stillness of the thick, polluted lake.

The area had been abandoned for at least a decade. Tangled grass had grown up over the path. Caribou moss wrapped around the bushes like thick grey beards of grumpy old men. The boathouse, ratted and unstable, was battered from years of storms and neglect.

"C'mon, Kanika!" called Panama. "Everyone's here."

"Who's everyone?" Kanika picked up speed in an effort to keep up. Before she had a chance to leap across the swampy patches between her and the boathouse, Panama was already at the door. As she swung it open, Kanika could hear screams of laughter and fast talk coming from the tiny shack. Through the streak of light blazing through the wide crack in the door, Kanika could see Gabe with a bunch of teenagers. She didn't know any of them.

"Panama!" Kanika called her friend to come back. But Panama stepped inside, grinning widely. Kanika watched as Gabe grabbed Panama around the waist and stuck his tongue in her mouth. One of the other guys appeared in the doorway.

"You coming in here? Or you gonna stand out there like a Black statue?" the guy shouted.

Kanika froze.

"Forget you!" the guy said. He slammed the rickety door shut.

Kanika backed away. She pivoted on her feet and ran back through the woods as fast as she could. Her heart was pounding and her legs were like jelly. But she couldn't stop running. Something wasn't right with what she saw. She wasn't sure what it was. What she did know was that she had to get out of those woods and back home.

Kanika stepped over the rusted guardrail. She sighed as she eyed Panama's bike leaning on it. The walk back along the dusty dirt road was long and tiring. A few cars passed Kanika along the way. But the drivers either kept right on driving or stuck an arm out of the window to wave at her. No one stopped to offer her a ride. It was just as well. She didn't want to have to explain where she had been or what she had seen.

It was close to dusk when Kanika began to speed up her steps. She kept hoping that Panama would come whizzing by on her bike and stop to pick her up. But by the time Kanika was just steps away from her front door, there was still no sign of Panama. Kanika sighed as she slipped inside for the night.

Chapter 3

Crying Eyes

The sun peered through Kanika's bedroom window early. As soon as it hit her eyes, she rolled over. She turned her back to the light, pulling the burgundy quilt up over her head. Her quilt was too thin to block the sounds coming from down the hall. She could hear water running from the kitchen tap. Then came the sounds of dishes splashing and clacking in the water. Several minutes later, Kanika heard the rhythmic swishing of the broom across the old kitchen tiles. There would be no falling back asleep.

Kanika became annoyed. She threw the quilt off and sat up in bed. She paused and listened to see if Aunt Becky was finished cleaning. For a moment, there was silence. Kanika smiled and eased back onto the pillow. Seconds later, the vacuum cleaner roared through the house, drowning out her thoughts. Kanika slipped out of bed and stomped down the hall. The vacuum got louder as she neared the living room. She stood in the doorway with her arms crossed. She watched Aunt Becky fiercely push the vacuum cleaner over the thick beige carpet.

"Good morning, Aunt Becky." Sarcasm dripped from Kanika's voice.

"Child, why you up so early?"

"Too much noise. Too much light in my room."

"Well, go climb into my bed. It's nice and dark in there."

"Can I just get something for breakfast?"

"Go on, sugar."

The phone rang as Kanika disappeared into the kitchen.

"Hello?" Aunt Becky sang out as she switched off the vacuum.

Kanika grabbed a bowl from the cupboard and filled it with cereal. She tossed three big spoons of sugar on top and doused it with skim milk.

"No word yet? Do they have any leads?"

Kanika could hear Aunt Becky faintly from the kitchen. She stopped mid-chomp to hear more. What leads? What was she talking about?

"No, I haven't mentioned this to Kanika yet. Not sure if she knows," Aunt Becky said in a quiet voice. Kanika slithered from the table to get a better listen at the kitchen door.

"But I don't want her to worry," Aunt Becky pleaded. "Look, I'm so sorry, Leslie. But I really can't help you. I'm already having so many issues with Kanika, I just don't want her involved in any of this."

Kanika jumped back to her seat when she

heard Aunt Becky saying her goodbyes. She couldn't finish the cereal. She wanted to know why her name was mentioned.

"Kanika!" Aunt Becky appeared in the entryway. "Got any plans for today?"

"Maybe." Kanika formed circles in the cereal with her spoon.

"Where were you yesterday?"

Kanika was not about to let her aunt know about the secret hideout. She figured Aunt Becky knew the boathouse was there. But she was sure her aunt had no idea that kids were hiding-out beyond the dead-end gravel road. She and Panama swore never to tell. Panama hadn't kept her word, but Kanika was determined to keep hers.

"Just went down the road," Kanika answered sharply.

"Alone?"

"Yeah, I guess."

"What do you mean, you guess? Were you by yourself or not?"

Kanika wondered why her aunt was pressing her. She'd never asked so many questions before. "I was with Panama for a while on her bike, that's all."

"And then?"

"I said that's all. I was with some of the kids at the end of the road. And Panama went somewhere on her bike."

"Where did she go?"

"I don't know, Aunt Becky. Oh my god, really?"

"Fine, I'm sorry. Finish your breakfast."

Kanika grabbed the bowl and dropped it in the sink. She left the kitchen and went to her room to get dressed. She thought about how Panama had been getting into trouble lately. She wondered if Panama got into any trouble when she got home the night before. They hadn't talked since they got to the hideout. Kanika was sure she would get a call from Panama at some point, bragging about her adventures in the boathouse. But by late evening, Kanika still hadn't heard from Panama. She didn't dare call. If Panama were in big trouble, then calling her house would surely make it worse.

Kanika convinced herself not to worry. But she did want to know why Aunt Becky mentioned her name on the phone that morning. Kanika had been wondering why she hadn't heard from Panama, and now she needed to ask. Aunt Becky was working away at a crossword puzzle when Kanika entered the living room.

"Hey, Aunt Becky, I heard you on the phone this morning."

"Oh?"

"Who were you talking to? I thought I heard my name."

Aunt Becky sighed and looked up from her puzzle book. "It was Leslie, Panama's mom."

"What did she want? And why were you two talking about me?"

"We were talking about Panama. She's missing."

"Missing?" Kanika was shocked.

"Her mother was hoping you knew where she was."

Kanika became angry. Why wouldn't her aunt tell her about this after the phone call?

Aunt Becky could see Kanika was upset. "I'm sorry, Kanika. I don't want you involved."

"Panama is my friend!"

"When I talked to you yesterday, it didn't seem like you'd been around her. So I didn't bother to bring this all up. There's nothing we can do here."

Kanika couldn't believe her ears. Why was her aunt acting so cold? "But I'm scared for Panama. I hope she's okay. Maybe I should talk to her parents."

"Do you know something?"

Kanika was so angry with her aunt she refused to share. If she was going to reveal their hideout to anyone, it would be Panama's parents. Kanika knew they wouldn't be happy to find out about the hideout and what Panama was doing there. She had to think very hard about whether or not she wanted to tell on Panama. Especially after she told Panama how bad it was to squeal.

"You will stay here, Kanika," said Aunt Becky. "And I don't want you calling them on the phone, either. You're just a kid. The police have been called. So let them do their job and find her. Like I said, we can't do anything here."

Kanika jumped up and stormed down the hall to her room. She was worried and hoped nothing bad had happened to her friend. She felt guilty for taking off and leaving Panama alone. A good friend would not have left. Kanika started crying. If Panama was hurt, it would be all Kanika's fault for leaving her in the woods. Kanika cried for close to an hour.

That night, as she drifted off to sleep, Kanika felt a tight knot in the pit of her stomach. She hoped that Panama was okay.

Chapter 4

Missing

Kanika sat on her bed, flipping through pictures saved on her computer. She stopped when she came to those with Danny Waterman in them, just to stare at him for a while. She knew Danny had been at the top of his class. Without breaking a sweat, he would make A's on his tests. He would get praise from teachers on his papers. Besides his grades, he had another great asset. He was extremely good looking. He was tall, with wavy blond hair, a gorgeous smile and soft pink lips. Girls called Danny a sweet-looking smelt.

Danny seemed perfect to Kanika. She obsessed about how she could get close to him. She had heard some bad things, like how messed up his family was. Kanika didn't care. She used to drag Panama to Danny's football games, hoping he would notice them and smile. She was glad whenever he showed up at the hideout. But after football season, Danny and his mother had moved to Halifax, about three hours away. Danny came back some weekends to spend time with his grandparents. But even Kanika noticed that each time Danny came back to Guysborough, he seemed different. More mysterious. One weekend, someone asked him at the hideout what it was like living in Halifax. Danny said, "You wouldn't want to know." Kanika and Panama had talked about what he might have meant by that.

A whole day had passed since Kanika heard from Panama. Kanika felt like she had

to do something. When Aunt Becky stepped
out to attend a community meeting, Kanika
decided it was the perfect chance to catch
up with Panama. If she hadn't gone home,
maybe she was staying at the hideout. Kanika
slipped out to the garage and grabbed Aunt
Becky's old rusted bike. Kanika's almost-new
mountain bike lay against the wall. It had
been there since the back tire busted. Kanika
was still waiting for Aunt Becky to replace
it. She hoped no one would see her pedaling
Aunt Becky's rusted contraption down the dirt
road. But she had no choice. She needed to get
to the hideout. There was no way she would
make it there and back on foot before Aunt
Becky returned.

The sun was high as Kanika emerged from
the dark garage. She squinted to keep the glare
out of her eyes. She hopped on the bike and
picked up speed, her feet pedaling as fast as
they could. The sun was already beating down
on Kanika's curly ponytail. It would only get

hotter as she rode. In no time, Kanika had reached the rusted guardrail. Panama's bike was still there, leaning in the same place they had left it the day before. Kanika could feel that something wasn't right. But she stepped into the woods anyway, heading toward the hideout.

The sun cast beams of light through the trees and across her path. The only noise she could hear was her heart thumping under her shirt and the birds chattering in the branches. She got to the clearing and had the hideout in her view. Kanika started to relax. It looked abandoned. Maybe Panama had fallen asleep and was still inside, not aware that she missed the night. Kanika stepped across the swamp and neared the front door of the shack. She stopped short when she heard voices. One voice was Danny's. She couldn't make out the other. Kanika stayed by the door and leaned in to listen.

"I won't go to the police. I promise," Danny pleaded.

"Stop being a little sissy. You agreed to this. Now you need to carry it out."

Kanika stared at the outline of a boy as it slid across the tiny space. It was Gabe.

"How the hell did I get myself into this!" Danny yelled.

"I asked myself that in the beginning, too. But you can't get out. Those cats make sure they have something on you. It's too dangerous to chicken out. Besides, you're getting paid aren't you? What other job is going to keep your pockets fat like that?"

Just then, Kanika lost her footing and fell against the squeaky door. Both boys jumped.

"What the hell was that?" Danny hollered.

Kanika turned and ran as fast as she could. When she peered back, she saw the boys standing in the doorway. Gabe started after her. Kanika picked up speed and slapped the bushes out of her way as she ran. Her heart pounded. What would he do if he caught her?

"Get back here, you bitch! Let me see your face, coward!" he yelled.

Kanika ran faster. When she got to the guardrail, she leaped over it and hopped on her bike. Without looking back, she pedaled as fast as her bony legs would allow. When she finally ran out of steam, she peeked over her shoulder. No one was there. She was safe. She continued pedaling until she made it home and into the garage. Kanika slammed the door shut, as if to shut off any chance of Gabe finding her or the rusted metal on wheels. She was sure he didn't see who she was. But she was still shaken up. She went straight to her room and locked the door to catch her breath.

Kanika tried to digest the words she'd overheard. What trouble had Danny gotten into? Did it have anything to do with Panama being missing? Kanika was angry with herself for almost blowing her own cover. She was sure Panama had found herself in some kind of trouble. And now it sounded like Danny was in trouble, too. Kanika grew angry. It seemed as if Gabe was behind it all. Kanika knew he was a no-good creep. But he was her only connection to finding out what had happened to her friend, and what kind of mess Danny was tangled up in. Gabe wasn't a good person. And Kanika was afraid of him. She didn't dare walk up to him and demand answers. Instead, she needed to come up with a plan. She needed to find Panama and help Danny. In order to catch Gabe out, her plan had to be a good one.

Chapter 5

Being Brave

Kanika was up extra early the next morning after not sleeping much the night before. She had been up half the night thinking about Danny and Gabe. Maybe Danny was trying to find out what happened to Panama and got caught up in the mess. He must have wondered why the girl who had brought him to the hideout in the first place was nowhere to be found. He must have noticed Panama's bike on his way into the woods. From what Kanika had heard the day before, it sounded like Danny was in a corner. Kanika had to come up with a plan to get closer to Danny to find out what he knew. That was the only way she could help Panama.

Aunt Becky was in her room getting dressed for church. Kanika knew she would be leaving in less than an hour, then staying afterward for a choir rehearsal. That would give Kanika at least four hours alone to figure out some things. The day she left Panama at the hideout, Kanika hadn't called Panama's parents for fear she would get her friend in deeper trouble. But Kanika knew Panama's parents. She knew they would be crushed about Panama's disappearance. They would wonder why their daughter hadn't called. They probably had many questions to ask Kanika. They were sure to ask for anything she knew that might help them figure out what happened to their daughter. Kanika knew she needed to call Panama's house.

A loud tap on her bedroom door shook Kanika out of her thoughts.

"Kanika, are you up?" Aunt Becky called

from the other side of the door. She jiggled the knob to see if the door was locked.

"Unlock this door, Kanika. You coming to church?"

"No, Aunt Becky," Kanika shouted. "Not coming this week."

Kanika hustled out of bed and opened the door. Aunt Becky barged in. Her eyes darted around the room. What did she expect to find, Kanika wondered. A boy? Drugs?

"Why you locking your door?"

"I locked it when I was changing last night. I just forgot to unlock it."

"You're acting mighty strange, Kanika. Not answering questions, locking yourself in this room. You went to bed without saying a word last night."

"What did you want me to say, Aunt Becky?"

"I don't know. How about goodnight?"

"Goodnight." Kanika smiled.

"Very funny. I wish you would come to church. Pastor Spalding has a special guest for the sermon this morning. He's from Texas.

And I know this man's gonna tear that pulpit up! It's gonna be good, girl!"

"Well, say a prayer for Panama then."

Aunt Becky's face softened. "Okay, Kanika."

Aunt Becky left, closing the door gently.

Kanika dressed and waited until she heard Aunt Becky's car thumping out of the driveway. She ran to the living room window and peeked through the curtains to see the tail end of the gold Ford Taurus leaving its dust on the pavement. Kanika plopped herself in the big armchair next to the phone. She was nervous as she dialled the number to Panama's house. The phone rang three times.

"Hello?" The soft voice came just as Kanika was about to hang up.

"Ms. Leslie?"

"Kanika?"

"Yes, it's me."

"My god, Kanika. I'm so happy to hear from you."

Kanika hadn't planned what she would say

before she called. She tried to find some words.

"So, you know Panama hasn't come back?" asked Ms. Leslie.

"Yes," Kanika replied.

"Have you heard from her?"

"I wish, but no."

Leslie sighed on the other end of the phone.

"I really miss her," Kanika said.

"Me too. If Panama contacts you, Kanika, you need to tell me right away. Okay?"

"Okay."

"You know, I spoke to your aunt the other day. She didn't think I should talk to you about it. Does she know you called me?"

"Yeah, she knows," Kanika lied. "But why didn't she want you to talk to me?"

"Well, with the stuff she went through with your parents and all. Maybe she didn't want you to feel responsible. But I needed some answers. I'm glad she came around and finally let you call me. We need to keep in touch for Panama's sake. And if you hear or see anything, like I said, please, please call me right away."

"I will. I promise." Kanika wanted to ask what Leslie meant about her parents. But she didn't know how.

"Okay, we'll talk soon, Kanika."

"Okay."

"Kanika, there is a number I think you should have."

"Whose number is it?"

"He's a police officer. He's trying to help us find Panama."

"Ms. Leslie . . ."

"Don't worry, Kanika, it's fine. If you don't feel comfortable . . ."

"I don't think Aunt Becky would want me to talk to the police."

Leslie sighed again. "Yes, I know. That's what she told me. I thought maybe she changed her mind. It's really important for you to talk to him, Kanika. You may have some tiny detail about that day. Something you don't even know you know. It could help us find Panama."

"Okay, I'll take the number." Kanika was terrified to take the number, and even more afraid to call it. She grabbed a pen and scrap paper from the side table. She jotted the number as Leslie recited it.

"Thanks, Kanika," Leslie said when she was done. "And everything's going to be all right."

"Bye."

Kanika hung up the phone. She wasn't sure what to feel. She wanted to help Panama. But she was scared to talk to a detective. What if she got in trouble for not telling what happened sooner? She wasn't sure exactly what she overheard between Danny and Gabe. What if it had nothing to do with Panama and she got Danny into deep trouble? Kanika didn't know if she was even ready to tell adults about the hideout at all.

Kanika took the number to her room. She hid it in a notebook in her top drawer. She wasn't sure that she would ever use it.

Kanika sat on her bed and thought about her talk with Leslie. Leslie had mentioned Kanika's parents. It sounded like she knew something Kanika didn't. Kanika was confused. Her mom and dad had both died when she was five, and Kanika had always wondered about them. What were they like? How did they die? Aunt Becky never talked about it. She had shown Kanika photos of her parents just one time. The photos showed them holding Kanika as a baby. Walking with her in the park. Standing over her as she blew out the candles at her third birthday party. As Kanika stared at the pictures, she imagined what they must have been like. She wished she could remember them.

Aunt Becky had once told Kanika how much her mother used to spoil her. She would buy expensive clothes and toys for her baby. Aunt Becky had sounded annoyed as she spoke about it. Since Aunt Becky never seemed to want to speak of Kanika's parents, Kanika wanted to know even more.

Kanika had many things she wanted to know about her parents. But it never seemed like the time to ask.

Chapter 6

That First Kiss

Kanika rummaged through her closet. She was looking for something that would grab the attention of a boy. She wanted to wear something more than the leggings and shirt she normally wore. Sasha, a girl at school, had asked Kanika to come to the community dance with her and her boyfriend Roger. The dance was like a kick-off to the start of summer. Vendors would be outside selling BBQ and sweets. Old man James Gorman would be out with his horse and buggy, charging two dollars for coach rides. And there would be door prizes. Kanika was very excited. Danny would certainly be there. This was the perfect chance for Kanika to get closer to him.

She didn't plan to ask Aunt Becky if she could go. She already knew the answer would be no. She would tell her aunt she was spending the night at Sasha's. The year before, Kanika had gone to the dance with Panama and Sasha, who was new to Guysborough. The three girls ended up having a really good time, even though Kanika almost got caught when she was sneaking back into the house after the dance. This year, Panama wouldn't be there to join them. But Kanika felt as if she had to go for her friend.

Sasha had been dating Roger for over a year. Roger was older than Sasha and in charge in their relationship. Anything Roger wanted Sasha to do, she did without question. Even when she didn't want to. Even when it may not have been the right thing to do. Sasha kept telling everyone that, when it came to Roger, she was a "ride or die chick." Kanika wondered what that really meant.

Kanika finally pulled a short purple skirt from the back of her closet. She looked it up and down and decided it would do. She ripped a tight white top from its hanger and tossed both pieces on her bed. She grabbed her book bag and stuffed the clothes inside. When she left her room, Aunt Becky was reading at the kitchen table.

"I'm leaving now," Kanika announced.

Aunt Becky looked up from her book. "And where are you going?"

"To Sasha's. Remember I told you last week?" Kanika lied.

"No, I don't remember that."

"So, can I go?" Kanika asked impatiently.

"I don't know, Kanika. I don't really know Sasha all that well."

"Don't you think I need to get out and be around people my age? It's hard with Panama gone, you know."

Aunt Becky gave in. "Yeah, I guess you're right. You should go."

Kanika smiled and kissed her aunt's forehead. "Thanks!" she sang.

Kanika ran to the edge of the driveway to wait. Roger drove a small car with a very loud engine. Kanika told Sasha that he needed to stop a few houses before hers so that her aunt wouldn't see who was driving. When she saw the blue bug creep up to the driveway next to theirs, Kanika ran toward them and hopped in. *Freedom* was the word that came to her mind as the car sped away.

* * *

Roger pulled up to the community centre, and they had to circle the parking lot three times before they could find a spot. The place was packed. Kanika couldn't wait to get inside. She was glad to be with Sasha. Sasha had been to the hideout plenty of times. Roger had been there too. A few times Roger wasn't with Sasha, but with other girls. A few times, Sasha asked him after hearing about the other girls. But each time he would lie his way through it and she would believe him. People thought Roger went out with Sasha just because of her father. Sasha's dad was in real estate. He owned apartment buildings in Halifax and had a lot of money. Anything Roger asked for, Sasha would buy for him. But she would always say she did it because he was her man.

Roger slammed the car into park and hopped out. He was nearly at the door by the time Sasha and Kanika caught up to him. Roger went inside without holding the door for them. So the girls took their time and walked in together. With people packed into the centre like sardines, it was hard to get a good look at who was there.

"Crazy in here, isn't it?" Sasha shouted over the pounding music.

"Totally," Kanika hollered back.

As they weaved in and out of the bodies, Kanika followed close behind Sasha.

"Where are we going?" she asked.

"Just follow me." Sasha smiled. "You'll see."

Butts brushed up against Kanika, and hips booted her to the side as sweaty bodies spun and twirled to R. Kelly's "Happy People." Kanika almost lost Sasha in the mix, so she clutched the back of Sasha's red cardigan. When they reached the far end of the gym, Sasha loosened Kanika's grip on the sweater. She placed Kanika's hand inside someone else's. Kanika had to squint to see whose hand was wrapped around hers. It was Danny. Kanika was surprised and nervous. It was the first time she'd seen Danny since Gabe chased her out of the woods.

"Hey, pretty brown chocolate." Danny grinned. It was obvious he'd found a way to sneak in some alcohol. His breath couldn't lie.

"Hi, Danny." Kanika wasn't sure what she should say. Danny was her crush. And he was her way to find Panama.

Sasha turned to go. "I'm going to leave you two alone and find my Roger," she giggled.

Kanika hadn't shaken her nerves. She wasn't quite ready for Sasha to leave. "It's okay, Sasha. I'll come with you," she said.

"Why don't we all go?" Danny said as he followed the girls outside.

Sasha took them through the back door so they could bypass the adults hanging around out front. Roger and several other young people were standing just outside. Sasha rushed over to Roger and wrapped herself up in his arms. All of the others seemed to be paired up too. Kanika felt awkward.

"This your new girl, Danny?" one of the boys yelled.

"Yup, she is tonight." Danny beamed and wrapped an arm around Kanika's shoulder.

Kanika smiled. She had never been called anyone's girl before. It felt nice. Danny was eighteen. To have an older boy think of her as his girl. It was something Kanika had wished for out loud, hundreds of times over, as she and the girls had *boy talk* at the hideout.

For most of the night, Kanika stayed close to Danny. She tried to find the right words to say. He held her hand as they moved in and out of the centre. They would run in and dance to a good song, and then would run out again to join the others.

Kanika was convinced that Danny had no idea it was her that Gabe chased through the woods. He didn't mention a word about it and Kanika didn't dare bring it up. The night had her feeling strange, but in a good way. It became clear that tonight wouldn't be a good time to bring up Panama.

When the DJ called for the final song of the night, Danny led Kanika to the dance floor. She was tall for her age, so she fit nicely in Danny's arms. He nuzzled his face into her neck as they swayed. Kanika didn't want the song to end.

Toward the end of the song, Danny placed his face close to Kanika's. He wrapped both his hands around her face and leaned in to kiss her. Kanika closed her eyes. The kiss was long and soft and wet. Kanika never wanted it to end. She hoped she was moving her tongue right, and opening her mouth when she was supposed to. When the lights came back up, Kanika and Danny were still kissing. Kanika opened one eye to see Sasha and Roger standing next to them.

"Song's over, lovebirds," Sasha said. "Time to go."

Danny pulled away from Kanika. "I'll walk you outside." He smiled.

The four of them exited from the side door. They got to Roger's car first. Danny asked if Kanika would ride with him. As much as she wanted to, Kanika knew she couldn't. What if someone saw and told Aunt Becky? Danny gave Kanika one last kiss and slipped a piece of paper with his number into the pocket of her white hoodie. Kanika said goodbye. As she sped off with Sasha and Roger, she just couldn't get the smile off of her face.

Chapter 7

The Truth Comes Out

"Kanika, come out here now!" Aunt Becky was screaming at the top of her lungs.

Kanika rolled over. She looked at the tiny clock on the stand by her bed. It was only nine-thirty. She'd had a late night at the dance and returned back from Sasha's house very early in the morning. She just wanted to stay in bed and dream a little more about her time with Danny. Why couldn't Aunt Becky let her do that?

"Now!" The shrieks grew intense.

"Oh my god, I'm coming!" Kanika hollered back.

When Kanika finally got to the living room she saw Aunt Becky standing with her hands on her hips.

"Child, I ought to slap you right straight into the middle of next week!" Aunt Becky said.

"For what?"

"You tell me!"

"Aunt Becky, do you know what time it is? Can I go back to bed?"

"Girl, you got five seconds to sit your narrow butt down on that sofa. You ain't going nowhere."

Kanika had no idea what had her aunt so angry. Did she find out about the dance? Kanika slid down on the sofa.

"What did you do at that dance last night?" Aunt Becky was standing over her.

How did she find out? Kanika wondered.

"I said, what did you do at that dance last night?"

"I don't know what you mean."

"Oh, of course you don't. Did you think I wouldn't find out?"

"I knew you wouldn't let me go."

"So you lied?"

"I'm sorry."

"So where did you spend the night?"

"At Sasha's, like I said."

"Oh, really?" The way Aunt Becky stared at her, Kanika could tell she was worried as well as angry. "Are you having sex, Kanika?"

"What?" Kanika was stunned to hear the word come from her aunt's mouth.

"Sex. Are you deaf? Or do you need me to say it in another language?"

"I'm not having sex, Aunt Becky."

"Oh, yeah? Then how do you explain what I found in your hoodie pocket?" Aunt Becky held out a condom in a bright green wrapper.

Kanika was shocked. Danny must have

slipped it in her pocket when he gave her his number. "That's not mine."

"Save your lies, Kanika! I want the truth."

"It's not mine! Someone must have put it there. For a joke."

"Well, this is not funny."

"Why are you so angry?" Kanika asked her aunt. "It's because you don't trust me. You think I'm lying about everything!"

"How can I trust you when you go out one night and come back with a condom in your pocket?"

"Get off my back! I haven't done anything wrong. If I wanted to, I could have stayed out all night and used that condom!"

Aunt Becky gasped.

"But I didn't," said Kanika. "Like I told you, I didn't even know it was there!"

"I'm just sorry I loosened my grip on you," said Aunt Becky. "I give you a small inch and you take a whole country mile. Just like your mother!"

The room grew silent.

"What does that mean?" Kanika finally said.
Aunt Becky didn't respond.

Kanika lashed out in anger, tears bursting from her eyes. "I asked, what does that mean? Why would you say that about my mother?"

Without saying another word, Aunt Becky turned and left the room. Kanika picked up the TV remote and threw it at the wall. She jumped up from the sofa, ran to her room and slammed the door behind her.

Kanika and Aunt Becky barely said a word to each other the rest of the morning. Just before lunch, Kanika snuck out to the garage where Aunt Becky kept the boxes of things that had belonged to Kanika's parents. The dusty containers were stacked against the back wall, covered by years of memories and old dreams.

It took Kanika nearly an hour to move things out of the way and figure out which boxes were which. It took another hour to sift through old photos, clippings and trinkets. Kanika was hoping to find something, anything, about her parents. But she found nothing.

Filled with disappointment, Kanika began restacking the old boxes. Just as she placed the last cardboard box on top of the pile, a tattered brown envelope slipped through a tear in the bottom of the box. Kanika placed the box back on the floor. She sat on the floor next to the envelope.

Before opening it, Kanika slid her fingers across the front. It was sealed with old tape. She gently pulled the tape away from the dirty envelope. As she got closer to opening it, she kept repeating *please, please, please*. Would this last find tell her something?

Kanika reached in and pulled out a bunch of clippings and newspaper articles. As her eyes scanned them, she started to realize what they were. She couldn't believe what she was reading. Her parents' fate was spread out over those newspaper pages for all the world to see.

Kanika picked one up and read it, the slip of paper shaking between her fingers.

Prostitute and Pimp End Up Dead in Halifax Hotel Room

Like a scene from a horror film, broken
lamps and smashed glass tell the story of
a life gone wrong. Grace Adams, 22, was
a known prostitute on the Halifax stroll.
Sources say her boyfriend, Fredrick Turner,
23, was her pimp. A tip from the hotel
staff led police to room 413 of the Admiral
Hotel, where Adams and her boyfriend
were suspected of running a sex service.
A member of the Halifax Regional Police
posed as a "trick" and set up a call with
Adams. The couple realized they had been
caught, and a scuffle broke out. Shots
were fired. The officer suffered non-life-
threatening injuries. Turner was pronounced
dead on the scene. Adams succumbed to
her injuries at the QEII hospital. They leave
behind a five-year-old daughter.

Kanika stared at the pages. The words blurred as her eyes filled with tears. She felt sad for the life her parents had lived, and for the tragic way they died. And Kanika was the only one who didn't know. She couldn't understand why her aunt had kept it from her. Why hadn't she just told her? It felt like a betrayal. Kanika had no idea how to deal with this new knowledge.

The honking of a car horn jarred Kanika out of her thoughts. She stuffed the article back into the envelope and hid it under one of the boxes. She would have to come back to it later.

Chapter 8

The Ride

Kanika was pleased to see Danny sitting in his
car at the end of the driveway. She thought
it was really bold of Danny to pull into the
driveway and honk. Luckily, Aunt Becky was
napping and hadn't heard the horn outside.
After everything she had just found out,
Kanika needed to get away from the house.
She needed to get away from Aunt Becky.

"Hop in," Danny called to her.

Kanika shut the garage door and skipped

over to Danny's car. She blushed when he smiled at her. *I guess I'm still his girl,* she thought to herself. *It wasn't for just last night.*

"Wanna go for a ride?" Danny grinned at her.

"You have to ask?"

Kanika hopped into the passenger seat. She grinned back as Danny did a half donut and peeled away from the house. All Kanika could see from the side mirror was dust and smoke from the gravel road. As Danny sped up, Kanika thought his driving skills were incredible.

Danny reached out for Kanika's hand. She reached over and laid her hand across his. They chatted and laughed, holding hands as Danny drove. Even if they hadn't exchanged a word, the way he looked at her said everything Kanika wanted to hear. She forgot all about Panama. She almost forgot about what she found out about her parents. All she could think of was Danny.

Danny drove through Guysborough until it was a faraway scene in the rearview mirror. It was a nice day for a drive, and Kanika didn't care where they were going. She was just excited to be along for the ride.

Danny pulled in at a tiny hut on the side of the road. An old woman was selling scoops of ice cream for a dollar-fifty each. Danny told Kanika it was his favourite place to get ice cream. They got out and ordered two large scoops each. Kanika had Moon Mist and Danny ordered a scoop of strawberry and a scoop of chocolate. Kanika squished up her face at Danny's choices.

"I like my sweet things to be chocolate." Danny laughed, winking an eye at her.

Kanika knew he was referring to her being Black.

"Your skin is so beautiful," he said.

Danny led her to the side of the hut where there was a worn-out picnic table. He climbed through on one side and she climbed in across from him. They gazed into each other's eyes as they hurried to eat their melting cones. Danny was finished long before Kanika so he just sat and stared at her. Kanika was self-conscious about him watching her. She was careful with every bite. She knew Danny could tell she was nervous, but he continued to stare.

"Ever had a boyfriend before?" Danny finally asked.

"Of course," she lied. She didn't dare say no.

"I mean a real boyfriend."

"Sure, kind of."

"Naw, I'm not talking about those little bitch boys at your school. They're just cubs. I'm talking about getting with a real man."

Kanika was excited by the fact that Danny was older. She was dying to know what it would be like to be with him.

When Kanika finished her ice cream, they thanked the lady and headed back to the car. They continued to make their way through town. After a few minutes, Danny veered off onto a winding dirt road.

He must have seen Kanika's confused look. "A friend of mine lives here," he explained. "He's working in Halifax for five days. So we can chill out here for a bit and watch some TV."

Soon they had parked and were inside the tiny bungalow. Danny started kissing Kanika eagerly. She kissed him back. They stretched out on the sofa, holding each other and kissing. They watched movies until dark. Danny asked Kanika to stay for the night. He promised to drive her back home in the morning.

Kanika thought about how angry she was with Aunt Becky. She thought of how much she wanted to erase what she had read in that newspaper article.

"Okay, I'll stay," she said.

Danny smiled as he led Kanika to the tiny bedroom. The only furniture was a freshly made single bed, a small nightstand on either side of the bed and a tall dresser in the corner of the room. There was a full-length mirror attached to the wall by the door.

Kanika's hand shook inside Danny's.

"Don't be scared," he said gently. "I won't hurt you."

Danny laid Kanika across the bed and pulled her shirt off over her head. He kissed her lips and neck. Kanika knew what they were going to do. She was afraid, but at the same time, she wanted it to happen. Soon they were both naked. Danny pulled down the blankets and joined Kanika in the bed.

Even though Danny kissed and caressed her, Kanika felt pain as Danny tried to enter her several times. But as soon as he was inside her, she felt tingling all over her body. She stared at the mirror. In it, she watched Danny's body rising and falling on top of hers. The sweet smell of his cologne filled her nostrils. Kanika grabbed Danny's hair as he breathed heavily in her ear. He whispered that he loved her and that he would always take care of her.

When it was finished, Danny rolled over to her side. "Are you okay?" he asked.

"Yes."

"It was your first time."

"Yes." Kanika was embarrassed.

"Don't worry, you're all woman now."

She smiled as Danny kissed her cheek. He rolled over and closed his eyes, but Kanika couldn't sleep. She lay there and replayed the event over and over in her head as Danny snored beside her. *You're all woman now.* The words echoed in her mind as she finally drifted off to sleep.

Chapter 9

Loyal

Kanika woke up just as the sun began to rise. She had had sex for the first time, and it had been with Danny. Kanika felt different from how she had felt any morning before. Life for her felt *different*.

"Let's go, beautiful. I need to get back to Guysborough," Danny announced. "Got some business to take care of this morning."

Danny's words sounded urgent. Kanika remembered the conversation she'd heard between Danny and Gabe at the hideout. Danny was probably being pressured by Gabe to do some things he didn't want to do.

Kanika gathered her things and slipped into the bathroom to get dressed. By the time she came out, Danny was already outside waiting in the car. He was tapping his fingers on the steering wheel impatiently.

"Don't bother locking the front door," he called out. "Nobody's going to come around here."

Kanika got into the passenger seat. She was quiet on the drive back, not sure how she felt about what she had done. How would she explain her overnight disappearance to Aunt Becky?

Kanika got caught up in her thoughts. She wondered if Panama had the same experience with someone. Kanika had mentioned Panama's name a few times as they drove around the day before. Each time Danny had ignored her or changed the subject. Maybe Panama had fallen in love with someone and never wanted to come back. Kanika paused to catch the word that had just bounced across her mind. *Love.* It was the word that described how she was feeling. She knew right then that she was in *love* with Danny.

* * *

The next two weeks were like being in heaven for Kanika. Aunt Becky argued and fought with her every time she saw Danny's car pull into the driveway. But Kanika fought back hard to be with him. There was nothing Aunt Becky could say to make Kanika give up the world of happiness she had when she was with Danny.

Danny treated Kanika extra special, taking her places, buying her things. She sometimes wondered what he saw in her. She was a few years younger than he was. Surely he could have his pick of pretty girls his age or older.

But he assured her that she was no longer like the other girls her age. She had become a woman.

"If you're going to be my official girlfriend, there's things I'm going to expect," Danny informed her. They were sitting in his car one night.

Kanika wanted to do whatever it took to please Danny. She was in love with him, and she was sure he was in love with her, too.

"I'll do anything." She smiled.

"So . . . would you dive off a cliff into freezing water?" He grinned.

"Sure." Kanika laughed.

"Would you let a rat walk all over you?"

"Eeew, I hate rats! I'm scared to death of them!"

"So, you wouldn't do that if I asked you to?"

"Well . . ."

"Yes or no, Kanika? I can't be with no girl who can't fall in line."

"Okay. Yes, I would do it."

"Good." Danny smiled and jumped out of the car. Kanika watched through the mirror as he went around to the back and popped the trunk. Within seconds he reappeared in the driver's side. He had a black box in his hands.

"What's that?" Kanika asked. She was afraid to hear the answer.

Danny lifted the lid from the box. Three rats scurried around inside. Kanika gasped and screamed. Danny laughed out loud. Kanika grabbed the door handle. Danny held her arm and pulled it away from the door.

"You just said you would do this for me."

"But I didn't mean for real!"

"Oh, I see. You're still just a kid. Sorry, that's not what I'm looking for. I guess I was all wrong about you."

Kanika felt awful. As horrified as she was by what Danny was asking her to do, she couldn't let him break up with her. She wasn't sure if she would ever get another chance to show him he wasn't wrong. She wanted to prove that she was everything he thought she was.

"No, I'll do it." Kanika squeezed her eyes closed.

"That's my girl."

Kanika kept her eyes shut tight. She squirmed and shook as Danny took the rats from the box. When he laid them on her, she screamed inside. She didn't dare open her mouth. One of the rats scurried up her chest and toward the back of her neck. Her eyes were squeezed shut. But she could tell that Danny was grinning with cruel enjoyment. Was this a sick part of him that she had missed? Or was it really his way to be sure that she really loved him? Kanika hoped it was the second one. She hoped Danny would realize that he already had her heart, no matter what.

The nightmare was soon over, although it felt like forever to Kanika. Danny finally peeled the rats from her body. He laughed out loud as he stuffed them back in the box.

"You're tough as shit, Kanika," he giggled.

He hopped out to place the box back in the trunk.

Danny stopped the car at the end of Kanika's driveway and turned toward her. He kissed her and wrapped his hands around her face. She could feel his warm breath on her cheeks as he talked.

"Kanika, you showed me today that you are a ride or die chick. Now I know I can trust you with anything."

His voice was smooth. Kanika had heard those words before. Sasha said she was Roger's *ride or die* girl. Kanika smiled. That was exactly what she wanted to hear.

"You *can* trust me," she said. "And I hope now you see how much I love you."

"I think so," he replied. "You can do a bit more to *really* prove it to me. But there will be lots of time for that."

Danny's hands slipped away and back to the steering wheel. Kanika exited the car and walked slowly up the driveway. She wasn't sure how to feel. She had started getting close to Danny to help Panama. Instead, she had fallen for him. Now, she was in love. Danny made her feel great, and she *wanted* to be sitting in that passenger seat. At the same time, she felt bad sitting next to him when he might know something about Panama that he wasn't telling her. She hadn't forgotten about Panama. But her feelings for Danny had taken over and she had no idea how to stop them.

She thought about talking to Sasha about it. Sasha was dating an older boy and seemed to know how to hold onto him. But Danny always got annoyed when Kanika mentioned her friends. Kanika decided against calling Sasha. Kanika's birthday was coming up in a few days and Danny promised to plan something special. She didn't want to spoil his surprise. Maybe she wouldn't mention Panama anymore until after her birthday.

Chapter 10

Bittersweet Sixteen

It was Kanika's sixteenth birthday. Danny's car pulled up to the end of the driveway. He leaned out and kissed her.

"Got that surprise for you." He grinned.

"I like surprises," Kanika responded.

"There's a wicked party happening in Halifax. I'm taking you with me."

"What kind of party?"

"A party, Kanika. What more do you need to know? I'm taking care of everything for our overnight. Think of it as your sweet sixteen."

Kanika was expecting a gift, not a party. But she had never been to Halifax before, so she was pleased.

"A party in the city. I love it!"

"Okay, I can't stay. I just wanted to pop by and let you know."

All Kanika could think of was walking into the party on Danny's arm. She couldn't get the smile off her face. Danny kissed her again.

"Gotta go! My grandfather's waiting on me to help him fix his van. So, pick you up tonight?"

"Can't wait!" Kanika stepped back away from the car and dashed toward the house. Inside, the hot food smelled amazing. Aunt Becky had prepared a huge feast of baked chicken with all the trimmings, and all the sweets Kanika could eat. Aunt Becky had invited some of her own friends over to celebrate Kanika's sweet sixteen and a few of Kanika's friends from school. Her aunt made it clear that it wasn't a *party*, just a small gathering to make her feel special on her birthday.

Kanika was happy to see Panama's parents there. Weeks had passed since Panama's disappearance and Kanika knew Panama's mom and dad were in a lot of pain. She was honoured that they had come by to celebrate with her.

Kanika had known that Danny wouldn't come inside. He wanted to keep him and Kanika on the down low, away from Aunt Becky. The dinner would be Kanika's pre-party to the real party in Halifax. Aunt Becky had no idea Kanika would be spending that night more than three hours away with Danny. And Kanika was not about to tell her.

After the guests had left, Kanika hummed the Mariah Carey song "Dream Lover," as she grabbed her best dress and overnight clothes. She packed them neatly in the bottom of her backpack. She scooped up a few toiletries from the dresser. As she zipped her bag shut, she could hear her aunt in the kitchen cleaning up. Kanika had already said goodnight, so she new Aunt Becky wouldn't be expecting to see her until daylight. Kanika quietly locked her bedroom door, grabbed her backpack and slipped out the bedroom window.

Since the house was one level, Kanika didn't have very far to jump. As soon as her feet hit the grass, she saw two flashes. It was the signal Danny had told her to watch for. Danny was early and impatient. Kanika hopped to an upright position and scampered across the lawn. Danny flashed the lights again. Kanika opened the car door to jump into the passenger seat. But a girl with long, straight blonde hair was already sitting there. She looked to be about seventeen. She gave Kanika a look and grabbed for the door handle.
It caught Kanika off guard.

"C'mon, get in," Danny demanded.
His voice was low and harsh.

Kanika hopped in the back and Danny

sped off. The drive to Halifax was filled with awkward silence. Danny turned the music up once they got on the highway. Kanika wanted to introduce herself to the girl in the front. But she wasn't sure if the girl would respond or ignore her. Kanika hadn't seen the girl around before. She would have remembered someone that pretty. She wondered if the girl was a cousin of Danny's or maybe somebody who just asked to hitch a ride with him to the party. She decided to wait. She could figure it out once they arrived in Halifax.

Kanika dozed off a few times during the drive. The glare of the city lights brought her out of her sleep. She sat up. There were so many buildings. Big houses lined the streets, row after row. It was nothing like the one house every quarter of a mile that Kanika was used to. The car turned onto Connaught Street, past a huge shopping mall. Kanika smiled. Maybe Danny would take her shopping in the morning.

From Connaught, they turned onto a smaller side street, and then another. Danny pulled into a driveway. Old, wide oak tree branches stretched across the paved lane, hiding a stucco house that sat at the back of the property. A black Lexus sat idly near the front entrance. The place looked deserted. If there was a house party going on, it must have been a horribly quiet one. And where were all the vehicles that the guests would have rolled up in? Kanika began to get a sinking feeling in her chest. She wondered what Danny was up to.

Danny glided his beater up alongside the empty Lexus. The blonde girl in the front seat looked over at him, waiting for instructions on what to do next. Kanika sat silently.

"Let's go," Danny said.

The girls left the vehicle. They both hesitated, unsure of what was happening. Danny rapped on the front door and then pushed it open without waiting. The girls followed. An older lady with curly brown hair appeared around the corner to greet them.

"Good, you made it," she said. "Bring them this way." Then she disappeared farther into the house.

It was obvious Danny had been there before. Kanika tugged on his arm as they followed the woman down a hallway and up a flight of stairs.

"What is this place?" she whispered.

"Just do what you're told and you'll be fine," he answered.

Once they neared the end of another long hallway, they entered a large back-room. The walls were painted the colour of dark red wine. Long black curtains were hanging from the window. There was a fancy wing-backed sofa and chairs set in one corner of the room, surrounded by expensive-looking vases and statues. On the other end of the room was a mahogany desk and chair. The only things on the desk were a phone, a notepad and a pen. The large bookshelf behind it was lined with books. They didn't look like anything that Kanika had ever seen or heard of. A young red-haired woman with big breasts got up from one of the wing-backed chairs as they entered.

"This is Kita," Danny announced. "She's gonna show you girls what's up."

Kanika looked at Danny. She was confused. Danny glanced back at her, noticing her fear. He leaned in and whispered in her ear, "You're a woman now, remember? You wanted that chance. Now prove your love."

Then Danny left the room.

Chapter 11

The Party

The red-haired woman took Kanika's purse away. The blonde girl, whose name turned out to be Crystal, tried to hide her tiny pouch inside her jacket. The red-haired woman patted her down then snatched the pouch. She took them down to the rec room in the basement and made them put on skimpy outfits.

"The party is about to begin," she told them. "And you two newbies are the main attractions. This is your breaking-in party.

And if you don't fall in line you will be seriously hurt."

She gave them each a glass of what looked like water. Kanika was thirsty, but it turned out to be straight vodka. Kanika gagged.

"Drink it down!" The red-haired woman grabbed the glass and forced it between Kanika's lips. Kanika coughed as the liquor stung the back of her throat.

"Here, take these," the woman said, holding out two tiny white pills. "They will relax you."

The girls took the pills. The woman made them open their mouths wide and checked inside to make sure they had swallowed them. Before long, Kanika began to feel dizzy. She felt like she was outside her own body. Everything seemed to be happening beyond her control.

The woman led the two girls to a dimly lit room at the back end of the basement. Kanika leaned on the bed, trying to regain herself. But nothing she did stopped the room from spinning. She could dimly see the outline of Crystal's body as it climbed on a bed across the room.

Almost right away, two men entered the room. One moved in Crystal's direction. The other stood over Kanika and pulled down his pants. Kanika felt weak. She didn't have the energy to fight him off. The man was aggressive and smelled like sweat. As soon as he finished with Kanika, another man entered. The scent of his cologne was very strong. Before Kanika could sit up, the second man was on top of her.

There seemed to be an endless stream of men for what felt like hours and hours. Kanika eventually stopped trying to resist and just let her silent tears flow. Several times she wanted to vomit.

In her mind she kept seeing images of her mother from the newspaper clippings. Had she experienced this pain? Kanika felt betrayed by Danny and sad. Had her mother felt the same kind of sadness when Kanika's father made her have sex with stranger after stranger? Kanika wondered how her father could be okay with it, her mother's body being used like an object. As Kanika lay sprawled across the squeaky bed, she finally felt a connection with her mother. Then she lost consciousness.

Kanika was unsure how long she had been asleep. But as she began to wake up, she could hear the red-haired woman screaming at someone.

"Stop letting those girls get in your head!" she yelled.

It was the wee hours of the morning. Kanika was naked and shivering. Her whole body ached. Danny had told her he was taking her to a party in Halifax. But what happened wasn't the kind of party she had imagined. She had all of her ID taken from her. No phone. No way to get back home. She looked over and saw Crystal.

"Hey," Kanika whispered loudly.

Crystal moaned and rolled over.

"Wake up," Kanika tried again.

"Why?"

"Do you remember me? Kanika. We drove here with Danny."

"Of course," Crystal said. She lifted her head and sat halfway up.

"I'm just trying to figure out what this is."

"We got raped last night."

Kanika pulled the thin blanket closer to her sore body.

"Over and over and over again," Crystal continued. "And all night long until we passed out."

"You passed out, too?"

"Yes, at some point. You ever drink alcohol before?"

"No."

"You ever take pills before?"

"Do you mean . . ."

"Drugs."

"No."

"You were pretty fried. I had to listen to

you screaming, begging the men to stop. A few of them slapped you so you would stop yelling."

"I remember." Kanika rubbed her cheeks. "It didn't seem real though."

"That's because we were drunk and high. Nothing seems real when you're like that."

"Does Danny know what happened to us?" Kanika asked. She was sure he would be upset.

"Does he know?" Crystal laughed. "Figure it out. He brought us here for this to happen."

"But he's my boyfriend." Kanika didn't want to think that Danny had set her up for this. But in her heart, she knew he had.

"Oh my god, you are stupid. All the girls here probably thought they were Danny's girlfriends, too."

Kanika's experience wasn't a bad dream. It was real. Danny had taken her to a strange place and dumped her like a bag of garbage. She had no idea how she would make her way back to Guysborough.

"I don't care!" The red-haired woman's voice grew closer.

"Do what you have to do to make this happen. And don't call me again until it's done!" The woman burst into the room. She was on a cellphone. She pulled the phone away from her face. "Get dressed," she ordered Kanika and Crystal. "Your drive will be here in fifteen minutes."

She threw a pile of clothes on the floor and left. Kanika pushed through the pounding in her head and got off the bed. She and Crystal sifted through the pile, taking what was theirs. She hoped her purse would be among the clothes, but it wasn't.

After they were dressed, Kanika and Crystal opened the rusted door. The red-haired woman had been standing there, waiting the whole time. She motioned for them to follow her upstairs. When they got outside, they saw a silver Jetta idling in the driveway.

The sun was just rising. With no clocks in sight, Kanika guessed it must have been around six in the morning. She felt hungry and exhausted. She and Crystal climbed in the back seat of the car. A blond man with a ponytail and another with a balding head and rotted teeth were sitting up front.

"Will we be able to stop for something to eat on the way back to Guysborough?" Crystal asked.

The two men looked at each other and started to laugh.

"Something to eat?" the man with the ponytail mocked.

"Guysborough?" the balding man behind the wheel repeated. They burst into laughter again as they peeled out of the driveway.

Crystal looked over at Kanika. They were both afraid.

"Buckle up, girls!" the driver shouted. "We've got a long drive ahead of us."

Chapter 12

A New Home

After about two hours in the car, Kanika and Crystal were asleep. Kanika wasn't sure where they were. But it was close to eleven when the men shook them awake. They led the girls into a fast-food place, ordered some breakfast for them and told them to use the bathroom.

"Do your business in the bathroom and don't be stupid," the blond one growled. "You've got two minutes to be back out here."

The girls hurried into the stalls. They came

out and splashed water on their hands. They didn't stop to dry them, just shook the water off as they left. The men were waiting outside the door for them.

"Get out to the car!" the men yelled.

On the way back to the car, Kanika noticed a sign just up the highway. It read Hotel Moncton. Kanika knew that Moncton was in New Brunswick. They were in a different province. She nudged Crystal and pointed out the sign. Crystal gulped. Who were these men and where were they taking them?

Kanika wanted to call Danny. There was no way he could have known that these men planned to take them out of the province. But as much as Kanika had pleaded in the past, Aunt Becky had never agreed to let her have a cellphone. Kanika wished now that she had been more persuasive. She remembered seeing Crystal use her phone on the drive in to Halifax.

"Let me see your phone," Kanika whispered.

"I can't. They took it from me last night, remember?" Crystal replied.

Kanika felt panicked. She had never been outside of Nova Scotia before. She had to find a way to contact Danny. But over the course of seventeen hours of driving, Kanika and Crystal remained in fear of their fate. They watched city after city pass by. The men kept a tight rein on them, never allowing the girls to leave their sight. The girls were fed well and they stopped for bathroom breaks. But the men were harsh in their talk and treated the girls like cattle heading to the slaughter.

When they pulled into a gas station on the highway, Crystal spoke up. "Do you think I can run in and call my mother just to let her know I'm okay?" she pleaded. "I promise not to say anything else. I just don't want her to worry."

The driver turned around. Without warning he backhanded Crystal across the mouth. Kanika jumped. Crystal cried as the blood gushed from her split lip. She held her hand to her mouth.

"Never ask me that again!" the balding man hollered.

Kanika helped Crystal clean her bloody lip with one of the napkins from their fast food bag.

It was almost morning the next day when they stopped at some place other than a gas station or a rest stop. The silver Jetta pulled up in front of a two-storey house surrounded by a rickety fence and overgrown bushes. The windows of the house were blackened and had bars. Kanika hadn't seen anything like it. But she figured the area must be dangerous enough to cause someone to install bars on the windows.

"Hellooo, Toronto!" the man with the ponytail shouted. He stepped out of the car to stretch his bones. "Well, Scarborough at least."

"Get out," was all the balding man said to the two girls.

Kanika and Crystal climbed out of the back seat and followed the men into the house. It was not what they expected. The living room was comfortable and had modern furniture. Kanika tried to get a sense of who lived there, but there were no pictures on the walls.

A tall, slim woman came walking from the kitchen. She wore a bandana on her head and had a long summer dress on. Kanika could see her long blonde locks bursting from the sides of the thin bandana.

"It's about time you jokers got here," the woman said to the men. "These the new ones?"

The men nodded.

She turned to Crystal and Kanika. "Welcome to your new home, young ladies. I'm Dawn."

New home? How could they expect Kanika and Crystal to live here?

"Well don't stand there looking like two dummies," she said sharply when neither girl answered. "You both know the deal by now.

Come on upstairs so I can show you where you will sleep."

The girls silently followed.

"There are a few items of clothing on the beds in your rooms," explained Dawn. "They may or may not fit. But you gotta make it work for now. Here's the rundown. You share this house with four other sex workers. You hos don't touch shit that ain't yours. You don't steal shit. You clean up your own shit. And you don't give me no shit. Follow that and you'll survive in here. Got it?"

Kanika and Crystal nodded fearfully. Kanika hadn't even heard the term "sex worker" before. Is that what she was now? But she knew she wasn't a thief. She had no plans to touch anything that didn't belong to her.

"I'm a sex worker, too. But I'm also queen bee," Dawn continued. "I'm the ho that keeps the rest of you bitches in line."

Dawn explained that the girls would be using hotel rooms to meet men, or tricks.

She said that someone would be nearby, waiting for them. She showed Kanika and Crystal a few signals to use if they needed help or if a trick pulled a weapon. She also told them how to set up tricks to rob them.

Kanika had a hard time taking in all the information. How was she supposed to go and have sex with strangers? Or rob them? The idea of having sex with dirty strangers for money terrified her. Kanika never knew a life like this existed.

As her mind wandered, she also wondered if this was how her mother ended up a prostitute. Had her father been someone like Danny who preyed on young girls and forced them into "the game"? Kanika became angry. She had thought Danny loved her. How could he make her do such things? Maybe her mother had loved her father, too. And he had forced her into a life that led to her death.

It was close to five in the morning when Dawn came into Kanika's room.

"The other girls will be making their way back soon," Dawn told her. "They'll be tired. So stay out of their way. You'll meet them in the morning."

Kanika nodded.

"Get used to this life," Dawn warned. "The boy got you in, and trust me, there's no getting out. So grow up fast. Or you'll be in for a world of hurt. This business is about money. You make it, you live. You don't make it, you'd better steal it or take the heat. Goodnight."

After sleeping what felt like only minutes, Kanika was awakened by Dawn. She was yelling for Kanika and Crystal to come downstairs. They made their way to the kitchen, where a bunch of girls were bustling around, preparing to eat breakfast.

"Meet the other girls," Dawn said.

Kanika scanned the room. Her eyes moved to the table and met the gaze of the skinny Asian girl painting her nails. Kanika slapped her hand over her mouth. It was Panama!

Chapter 13

Reunion

Kanika rushed to the table and parked herself in the chair beside Panama. She couldn't believe her eyes. Panama stopped painting her nails and stared into Kanika's eyes. They just looked at each other for a long time. Kanika read Panama's face. It was pleading for help. But Dawn was watching closely. Panama remained silent.

"How are you, Panama?" Kanika said at last. "I've missed you."

"Hi, Kanika," Panama replied softly.

"You two girls know each other?" Dawn inquired.

"Oh, yes. Panama is from Guysborough County like me. We . . ."

"Guysborough? What the hell is that?" one of the girls hooted.

"Sounds like some kind of back-woods hick town to me," Dawn said and laughed.

"It's in Nova Scotia," Kanika announced. "It's on the East Coast." Everyone except Panama and Crystal laughed at Kanika.

"You proud of that?" Dawn joked. "Girl, get the hell out of here with that east coast, Scotian shit. Don't nobody care where you come from. We only care that you don't be stupid and that you don't do anything to get all of our faces kicked in. You ain't no better than the rest of us. We're all trapped in this crazy-ass nightmare."

The other girls went about gathering their breakfast. Dawn left the room.

"Do you want to grab something and eat

it upstairs?" Panama asked. She motioned to Kanika. Kanika grabbed a bowl of cereal and followed Panama up to her room. Panama closed the door behind them. She set her nail polish down on the dresser and sat down on her bed. Kanika sat beside her.

Kanika knew Panama had a dark story to tell. And Kanika wanted to hear every word. Once Panama was finished, Kanika would tell a dark story of her own.

"You remember Gabe?" Panama started.

"Of course. The creep."

"He did this to me. He's the reason I'm here. They took me from the hideout that day, Gabe and three other guys. I thought we were going to Halifax to meet up with some of Gabe's friends. But it was a lie. He dropped me off at this scary house. He fed me to Dragon."

"Who is Dragon?"

"He's the pimp. He owns all the girls here. And he is very cruel. He has all kinds of young guys working for him, recruiting girls."

"That's what Danny did to me and Crystal."

"Danny fed you to Dragon?"

"Yes."

"Gabe and Danny are both recruiters. Danny was one of the guys who helped Gabe drag me from the hideout. Gabe smooth-talked his way into our little secret in the woods. It was only so he could find girls to give to Dragon. I can't believe there was a time when I said I wanted to marry him."

"I know." Kanika thought about Danny and her dreams of their life together.

Panama was near tears. "Kanika, it was so horrible what they did to me."

Kanika hugged Panama. She felt her pain. She had lived it, too.

"I tried to fight them off," Panama said. "But those boys beat me up so bad. I had a black eye and two broken ribs by the time those two thugs rushed me out of Nova Scotia. They wouldn't even let me go to a doctor. I was in so much pain."

"I promise, I looked for you, Panama," Kanika said. But she felt guilty. She started out to find her friend. But after getting caught up with Danny, she lost focus and fell in love. She had stopped looking for Panama.

Several hours had passed by the time Panama and Kanika finished talking. By the end they were both crying. Kanika was heartbroken to hear that Panama was dragged kicking and screaming from the hideout. Panama had been so frightened from that point on, that she never resisted the men again. Kanika wished she had stayed. If she hadn't been scared off by the boy, she could have been there to help her friend.

"And it doesn't get any better, Kanika," Panama explained. "I've watched girls get punished for not making enough money, or for causing a fight with other girls. It's even worse punishment if they try to leave."

"That scares me," Kanika said in a whisper.

"One of the girls here tried to leave. When

Dragon caught her, he beat her so badly that she didn't wake up for two days. He wouldn't allow any of us to touch her. I thought she was dead. When she woke up, she was lying on the floor in the same place she was beaten, soaked in her own dried blood."

"That's horrible."

"And whatever you do, don't come back without any money. Last week, one of them came back empty-handed because she got robbed. Dragon tied her up and burned her with cigarettes until she screamed for mercy. Then he sent her back out to make up the money she lost."

"But didn't Gabe try to stop this? And why would Danny do this to me? He was supposed to be my boyfriend."

"None of them were ever our boyfriends, Kanika. Danny gets paid really good money to find stupid girls like us for Dragon."

Kanika started to cry again. "I don't want this, Panama. I just want to go home."

"You have to be quiet, Kanika," Panama sniffled. "We don't want the other girls to hear us crying."

"I'm scared. I don't want to go out there tonight. What if I don't make any money? What if Dragon beats me until I die?"

Panama hugged her tightly. "It will be okay, Kanika."

A gentle knock on the door made the girls pull apart. They wiped their faces with the sleeves of their sweaters.

"It's open," Panama called.

Crystal peeked her head in the door. "Mind if I come in?" she asked.

When Panama nodded her head, Crystal slipped into the room and shut the door. She climbed up on the bed and crossed her legs. She looked down at her hands. But she didn't say a word.

"Everything okay, Crystal?" Kanika asked.

Crystal was trembling with fear. "My . . . my period started."

"Oh my god," Kanika said.

"What do I do?" Crystal pleaded.

"You've got to tell Dawn," Panama said. "They're gonna send you on all the creep calls."

"What's that?"

Kanika could tell Crystal was almost afraid to ask.

Panama explained, "They get really weird requests sometimes. People wanting to pee in a girl's mouth or do other crazy things. And some of them don't care if a girl is on their period."

"Eeew! That's frigging gross," Crystal moaned.

"It is, but they pay more money. So, it's bad but it's good, if that makes any sense."

What Panama was saying made Kanika feel nauseous. She knew that she couldn't stay. She decided that at her first chance, she would run away. She would get to a police station and ask for help.

Kanika told Panama and Crystal what she wanted to do. She asked them to escape with her. Crystal said no right away. She was too afraid of what might happen to her if they got caught. Kanika was sure her best friend would come along with her.

But Panama hung her head.

"It's not worth the risk, Kanika," Panama said. "You can't get away."

"But don't you want to make it home to your parents?" Kanika asked Panama. "They love you, and they miss you so much."

"And I miss them. But that's the thing. I will never make it home to them. And if I do, it won't just be my own life that will be in danger. Theirs will be, too. Dragon has guys everywhere, and will hurt people to get back what he thinks is his."

The room went completely silent as the three girls thought about their fate.

Chapter 14

The Game

In the month since Kanika arrived at the house in Toronto, days seemed to blend into each other. Kanika began to learn how things worked between the girls in the house. She had to figure things out on her own, as Panama was always out on trick calls. There were a lot of kinky men with sick fantasies of tiny exotic Asian teens.

It didn't take long for Kanika to find out that Dragon slept with the girls. On her very first day there, Dragon burst into her room in the middle of the night. Having Dragon force himself on her made Kanika want to vomit. But she was too afraid to resist him.

But there was one girl named Ru that Kanika had never seen Dragon treat like his property, to have sex with whenever he wanted. Ru always brought in a lot of money. But she was bold and sassy instead of scared like the other girls. Kanika talked to Ru as much as she could. Maybe she could figure out a way to avoid Dragon.

"Don't mess with Dawn, whatever you do," Ru warned Kanika. "She's Dragon's right hand. And she's as jealous as they come. She's a crazy bitch. She knows Dragon gets with all his girls. But if she thinks you actually want him, her claws will come out. If she thinks Dragon is taking a special liking to you, she'll slice you in a minute!"

Kanika found that news scary and strange. It seemed like everyone was Dragon's girlfriend, since he was everyone's pimp. But there was no love involved. The girls were scared of what Dragon might do. And Dragon acted like he owned all the girls. In what kind of world could one guy have all these girls any time he wanted to and nobody else could say a word about it?

"I've noticed that some of the girls seem jealous of each other," Kanika said.

"It's all about loyalty. They are all competing to show Dragon that they are the most loyal."

Kanika's talk with Ru was eye-opening. She tried to stay clear of Dragon when she could. She never wanted to be his favourite. She never wanted to be on Dawn's bad side. One evening, Kanika got a taste of Dragon's cruel wrath. She had been lucky and received a hundred-dollar tip from a trick. The trick was an older man and Kanika thought he probably felt sorry for her. She was relieved to have received such a tip, and she was sure Dragon would be pleased. Maybe he would leave her alone for a little while. But Kanika was in for a shocking surprise when Dragon counted out her money that night.

"Where did you get all this extra cash?" he growled.

"It was a tip."

"Like hell it was. You think I'm an idiot?"

Kanika was confused. She thought Dragon would be happy. But he was angry and she didn't know why.

"Answer me!" Dragon screamed.

Kanika had no idea what to say. She'd already told the truth.

Before Kanika could answer, Dragon hauled back and plowed his fist into her face. Kanika was stunned and the room went black. When she opened her eyes, she was on the floor. Panama and Crystal ran to her side to help her.

"I don't understand," Kanika said.

Panama whispered in Kanika's ear as she

helped her to her feet. "Did you sleep with a trick without a condom?"

"No."

"Did he ask you to?"

"No." Kanika steadied herself and rubbed her swollen cheek.

"Men usually give big tips like that if we agree not to use a condom. But Dragon forbids that. He doesn't want any girls with diseases."

"But I never . . ."

"Just hush, Kanika. Don't talk about it anymore. You're new and he knows you didn't turn enough tricks to make that much tonight. You have to figure out what Dragon thinks you will make in a night. Say you're having a good night for money and you get a crazy tip like that again. Just keep the tip and keep your mouth shut. But you'd just better make sure no one ever finds out about it."

That night, holding an ice pack to her bruised face, Kanika thought about what Panama had said. She was still learning all of

Dragon's rules. But Panama had given her an idea. She needed to find a way to get back with the older man again. She felt that the man sensed her desperation and would tip her again. If he kept giving her those kinds of tips, she could save up enough to finally get away.

Kanika talked about escaping often. Each time she did, Panama would change the subject. As much as she hated the life they were living, Panama was too scared to run. She never wanted to think about what would happen if she left with Kanika and got caught.

The swelling under Kanika's eye and cheek was just about healed when she met with the older man again. He looked concerned when he saw her face.

"Everything okay?" he asked. "Your guy scraped you pretty bad, huh?"

"Yeah." Kanika decided to play on his sympathy. "Didn't bring in enough money."

The man shook his head. He seemed disgusted by what Kanika was saying. Kanika glanced at his open wallet on the hotel nightstand. "Craig Pettrie," his driver's license read. Another quick glance and Kanika spotted red and brown bills bulging inside the wallet. By this time, Kanika knew they were fifty and one-hundred dollar bills. *There must be at least a thousand dollars in there*, she thought.

The first time Kanika was with Craig, he had spent all of the time talking. There had been no time left for anything else. Kanika hoped this time he would do the same.

"What do your parents think about your lifestyle?" he continued.

"I don't have any parents."

"Gosh, that's why you're doing this, isn't it?"

Kanika wasn't about to share her life's story with the stranger.

"Sorry to pry," he apologized as he pulled his pants down. Kanika was disappointed. She wanted him to run out the clock talking, but he was ready to get down to business. He noticed Kanika's hesitation.

"Don't worry, I'll give you a good tip."

With that assurance, Kanika dropped to her knees. At the end of her night, she slipped away to her room to hide the second hundred-dollar tip Craig had given her.

Kanika did the same thing every time she met with Craig. She managed to pull a space apart at the bottom of her wooden bedroom lamp. Every time, she slipped the extra money inside. She didn't tell anyone about the tips, not even Panama. Some things had not changed, and Panama was still the girl who was a rat under pressure. If Panama knew about Kanika's money and where it was hidden, she would spill all the beans to Dawn or Dragon. And Kanika couldn't risk that, even for her best friend.

Chapter 15

Ru

The weather was chillier than usual when Ru asked Kanika to go out with her one night. It was a robbery plot that Dragon had set up. The target was a high-profile lawyer. He was defending a businessman suspected of sexually assaulting three of his employees. Even Kanika knew that because it was all over the news.

The lawyer requested two young Black girls. Kanika was hesitant to go along. She didn't want to be involved in any robbery. Dawn told Ru and Dragon they were making a mistake by taking "an amateur like Kanika" along. They stood to make a lot of money, and she was sure Kanika would mess it up. But since Ru and Kanika were the only two Black girls in the house, Dragon didn't have much choice.

"Don't worry. I'll make sure she knows what to do," Ru assured Dawn and Dragon.

In the taxi, Ru talked in code so the driver wouldn't catch on. He glanced at them often in his rearview mirror. The way he looked at them creeped Kanika out.

Ru explained that since she had the most experience, she would occupy the lawyer first. She would make sure he was happy. Then Kanika could continue to entertain him while Ru stole his money. Kanika wasn't ready to do the actual robbing. They had worked out a signal for when Ru had the money and it was time to leave. It would be Ru asking the lawyer for a cigarette.

As they got out of the car in front of the hotel, Ru handed the driver a twenty-dollar bill.

"You lesbians have a good night, now!" he said. He winked at Ru.

"We will, you damn pervert!" Ru yelled back. She slammed the car door shut.

Kanika was shocked to think the driver thought she was a lesbian. But maybe it was better than everyone knowing the truth, that she was a sex worker. She thought back to her mother. Was her mother ashamed by how she lived?

The girls made their way up to the hotel room. Ru tapped on the door next to the one that the lawyer was waiting in.

"This isn't the right room," Kanika whispered.

Ru ignored Kanika. She took a key card from her pocket and slipped it through the slot. The light turned green and she walked in. Kanika followed. Dragon was already sitting

inside. He would be their protection
if the lawyer caught on and tried to hurt them.
The three couldn't be seen arriving together
in case the lawyer spotted them and became
suspicious.

"You ready for this?" Dragon asked
Kanika.

"I think so."

"Don't think so. *Know* so!" he snarled

"I'm ready," Kanika gulped.

"Good. Don't screw this up."

Kanika was scared to death. She hoped the
lawyer couldn't smell her fear. But everything
seemed to go as planned. After what seemed
like too long, Ru asked the lawyer for a
cigarette. It was done. When the lawyer told
Ru that he didn't bring his smokes, the girls left
the hotel room.

The girls made their way down the back
stairs. They waited there in case the lawyer
found he'd been robbed before they could leave
the building. Dragon pulled up around back,

tires squealing. The girls hopped inside his car. Kanika's heartbeat finally returned to a normal rate. She wondered how the girls at the house had been able to survive such danger for as long as they had.

Later, Kanika found out that Ru was able to get four-thousand dollars, a chequebook and a gold credit card from the lawyer's wallet. "Pay dirt," Ru called it. Kanika watched as Ru handed everything over to Dragon. He counted out the bills and handed Ru a bunch of the brown ones, a handful of hundreds. Kanika had never seen Dragon give any of the other girls money. If they needed something, he bought it. He didn't give away cash. Kanika needed to find out why. How was Ru different from the other girls?

A few days later, Kanika got her chance. She and Panama were at the kitchen table playing cards when Ru passed by.

"Can one of you hand me that laundry soap from up there?" Ru asked. "I don't know why these hos never put shit back after they use it." She was holding a basket of dirty laundry.

"I'll get it." Kanika hopped up from the table to retrieve the bottle.

Ru struggled to find a free finger to grasp the handle.

"I'll just bring it for you," Kanika offered.

She followed Ru to the basement. She set the detergent on the floor and watched as Ru piled her clothes into the washer. Ru turned and noticed that Kanika hadn't left.

"You still here, kid?"

"I wanted to ask you something."

"Well, ask."

"How come Dragon gave you all that money?"

Ru grabbed the soap from the floor to add to her wash.

"Because it was mine, stupid."

Kanika was puzzled. "How? Why wasn't the money all Dragon's? Why did he keep only some of it?"

"Because I pay him to protect me."

"Huh?"

"Gosh, you have a lot to learn. He's my pimp. I sought him out and he agreed to protect me. After I got caught up out on the streets, I knew I needed someone to watch out for me."

"But —"

"I'm not like you. I wasn't forced here. I came on my own."

"Why? Who would want this?"

"There are a lot of sex workers who chose to do this. It's their work. Just like teaching is work and picking up garbage is work."

"Don't you feel dirty doing this work?"

"No."

Kanika was surprised to hear the way Ru was talking. Kanika wanted to get out so badly. She never thought she would ever meet someone who *wanted* to be here.

"You're just like the rest of the chumps out there," Ru said. "Looking down on people like me as if your life was perfect. As if you were perfect before all this."

"I didn't say I was perfect."

"You don't have to. People like you piss me the hell off."

Kanika didn't want to make Ru mad. She tried to make it right. "I'm sorry," she said.

"For what?"

"For judging you. I didn't mean to. It's just that I don't understand this life." Kanika thought about her mother. Maybe she chose this, like Ru did.

"I don't get it," Kanika continued. "And I don't want any part of it. I just can't see how anybody would. I'm just trying to understand it, that's all. Aren't you a victim, too?"

"Girlfriend, I'm nobody's victim. Let me tell you something. What happened to you isn't right. I'm not down for that. Nobody should be forced to do anything they don't sign on to do. But it's different with me. This is how I make my money. I'm twenty years old. I've been a sex worker since I was eighteen. It was how I put myself through college. I got my certificate in cosmetology."

"So why are you doing this?"

"Because it's the work I chose. If I want to leave, I can give Dragon an exit fee and move on. But I make more in one day doing this work than I would in a month of putting makeup on people, day after day and telling them they look pretty. Here's what's so messed up about it. If someone makes porn, they're making money by using other people's bodies to have sex with each other. It's legal. But when a sex worker like me uses her own body, all of a sudden it's wrong."

"I still don't get it, Ru. This is a bad business."

"Look, what I do with my own body should be my choice. You may never understand it, Kanika, but don't judge me. Like I said, what happened to you was wrong. But I chose to get into this. And I can get out when I choose."

Kanika slowly walked back up the stairs. She understood the lure of money. But the things she'd seen and felt while being trafficked were horrific. She still couldn't imagine anyone wanting to be in this life. But she respected Ru's strength to make her own choices.

Panama was still sitting at the table when Kanika came back up. "What took you so long?" she asked.

"I have a headache, Panama," Kanika said instead of answering. "I'm going to lie down."

Kanika went to her room to be alone. She was left not knowing how to think. She stretched out across the bed. She wished that when she woke, she would be back home in her own bed.

Chapter 16

Come With Me

"Here, drink this."

Ru passed Kanika a hot cup of lemon-flavored cold medicine. Kanika had caught a bad flu. She had barely been out of bed in over a week. Dragon wasn't pleased about losing money, so he kept checking in on Kanika to make sure she wasn't faking. Kanika squished up her face when she saw the steaming cup.

Ru sat on the edge of the bed. "Take it," she insisted.

Kanika slowly sat up in bed. She felt dizzy. She shifted her body against the pillows and held her hands out for the cup.

"Careful, it's hot."

"Thanks." Kanika took a sip and closed her eyes. She hated the taste.

"What a wimp." Ru chuckled as she watched Kanika force a swallow. She took the cup from Kanika and set it on the nightstand. "Let it cool a bit. But make sure you drink it all. You need to get better."

"Why? I never want to go out and turn tricks ever again. I'd keep the flu forever if I could. I'm not cut out for this. I didn't ask for this, Ru. I just want to go home."

Ru sighed and got up to leave.

"But it's true," Kanika whined.

"I know." Ru left and closed the door quietly behind her.

Kanika slid back down in bed, hoping that she hadn't made Ru too mad.

Kanika hadn't dozed off for an hour before

noises in the hallway woke her. She sat up to
listen as the sound of arguing grew louder. It
seemed that one of the girls ratted to Dragon that
someone was hiding money. Dragon ran through
the house like he was on the warpath. He hollered
and threatened everyone. Kanika was nervous.
Did someone find the stash she had hidden in the
base of the lamp? If Dragon burst in and went
through her room, he might find her money. She
didn't even want to think about what he would
do if that happened. Her head throbbed.

"Just calm down, Dragon." Dawn was
pleading with him.

"You all better pray I don't find one hidden
penny!"

Kanika could hear Dragon burst into
Brittany's room across the hall. After a minute,
he came out screaming for someone to find
Brittany. Dragon had found a hundred dollars
taped to the back of a photo he ripped from her
wall. He stormed down the stairs, banging his
fist against the walls as he went.

Kanika lay back down and pulled the blanket tightly over her head. She wanted to be somewhere else. She didn't want to even hear what was about to befall Brittany. Kanika started to cry. It was only a matter of time before she would be found out, too.

The day stretched into the evening. Kanika cried herself to sleep. She was shaken awake by Panama. Panama looked awful. Her eyes were swollen as if she had been crying.

"What's wrong?" Kanika asked, still too drowsy from the medicine to pay attention.

"I figured you probably didn't know. Oh, Kanika it was awful. All we could do was watch. Poor Brittany."

Kanika wasn't sure she wanted to hear any more.

"Kanika," Panama went on. "Brittany's in the hospital right now. Dragon beat her so bad. One of the girls even laughed while Brittany screamed. Dragon threw Brittany down the stairs and left."

"Well, the police should arrest him!"

"Brittany will never say it was Dragon."

"Why not?"

"Think about it, Kanika. It would only make it worse."

Panama's words sent shivers through Kanika's sick body. Panama was right. And Kanika had money hidden like Brittany. She had been with Craig a few times, and what she had in her lamp was almost five-hundred dollars. The knowledge that she could end up like Brittany petrified Kanika. She suddenly felt as though she couldn't breathe. It felt as if someone was pressing on her chest and blocking her air.

"I have to go get ready for tonight," Panama said. She didn't seem to notice Kanika's panic. "I just wanted to let you know what was going on."

As soon as she left, Kanika got out of bed and rummaged through her drawers. She still didn't feel well, and the flu had really been taking its toll. But she knew she had to find a way out. Her hands were shaking as she grabbed clothes and stuffed them into a drawstring Adidas bag.

Kanika jumped when she heard a tap at the door. Without waiting for a response, Ru stepped inside. She caught Kanika trying to hide the bag under the blankets on her bed.

"Finally leaving, huh?" Ru said.

Kanika couldn't answer.

"I came up to see if you were going to make your move," Ru explained.

"How did you . . ."

"Panama told me you guys talked about Brittany. I figured that would have freaked you out."

"You won't tell the other girls on me will you?"

"You think these hos care if you take off? You'll just be one less girl they need to be jealous of."

"You're going to help me get out?"

"This life is rough, and you're a victim. With all your questioning, you're just going to make it harder for the rest of us. It's in my best interest to help you get away."

Kanika thought of Panama. Their chance had finally come to get back to Guysborough. They could return to the families back home worrying about them.

"Wait here for a minute," Kanika said. Ru started sifting through Kanika's bag to see what items she was trying to take with her.

Kanika stepped into Panama's room. She was excited that she finally had good news for her friend. Panama was sitting in a chair in the corner putting on mascara. She looked like an Asian beauty queen. Her deep, dark eyes looked even more mysterious when she dressed them with makeup.

"Kanika, you're feeling better?" Panama caught her eye in the mirror.

"Not really. I took a bunch of Tylenol though. I just came to take you with me."

"What are you talking about?"

"Ru is going to help us get home."

"That's not true. She would never do that."

"Are you coming?"

Panama continued to put on her makeup, not looking at Kanika. "You're crazy, Kanika. I think you want to die."

"Panama, this is our chance to go back home. Please, come with me."

Panama put down her mascara and looked up at Kanika. "Back home to what? Face it, Kanika. We're not the same people we were back in Guysborough. And how long do you think it would be before Dragon's goons found us there?"

Kanika's smile dropped.

Panama went on, "You think Dragon will say, 'Glad you made it home safe?'"

"So, you're not coming with me?"

"Hell, no. You're going to get caught. And then you're going to be in serious trouble. There's no way out of here. Ever."

Panama went back to her makeup. Kanika wanted to cry. But she held back her tears as she left Panama's room. She thought it would probably be the last time they would see each other. How did it come to this?

Chapter 17

Witness

Panama's decision made Kanika sad. But she had to think about herself. When she got back to her room, Ru had her things tossed across the bed.

"What are you doing?"

"You can't take this stuff, stupid. You can't take anything that Dragon bought you."

Ru began placing the clothes back in the drawers. Kanika grabbed a few ordinary rags that she'd bought for herself. Ru put them in the bag.

"And don't forget your money," Ru said.

How did Ru know she had money? Kanika forced a puzzled look.

Ru laughed. "Oh, you think I don't know you have money stashed away? I almost told on you a few times. But I felt sorry for you. You were so desperate."

"How did you know?"

"That old man always tips big. I'm the only one who knows, though. He always asks for a type. He likes chocolate girls, and the rest of the girls here don't fit. But, Kanika, it doesn't take long to catch on to anything around here. If those girls found out, they would run and tell right away. They would be happy to tell Dragon you've been stashing money just so they can watch you get your face punched off."

"That's why I need to get the hell out of here, Ru. Thank you for helping me."

"No, this is all you, girl. If you get to Nova Scotia, that's all on you. And if you get caught, that's all on you, too. If my name ever comes out of your mouth as having helped you, that'll be the last word you ever speak. You got that?"

Kanika nodded her head. The last thing she wanted was to get Ru in trouble. She had already opened her mouth to Panama. She prayed Panama wouldn't repeat Ru's name to anyone.

Ru was taking a huge risk to help her and Kanika knew it. Ru told her she had convinced everyone she was taking Kanika along to see a trick who wanted two black girls. They slipped out of the house and were soon driving through the city. Ru gave Kanika advice on how to stay safe in the streets.

"I'm going to get out at the next block," said Ru as they reached a corner. "So you'll be on your own from here. I've done all I can for you. Just remember everything I told you, okay?"

Kanika nodded. All of a sudden she was nervous. Without Ru, she wasn't sure she would be able to make it out of Toronto safely. She didn't know the streets like Ru did. And she had no idea how much time she had before Dragon realized she was gone and came looking for her. Soon, the car turned onto the next block. Kanika's heart pounded.

"You'll be fine." Ru smiled as she exited the taxi.

But as soon as Ru stepped out, three men appeared out of nowhere. It was Dragon and the two men who had driven Kanika and Crystal to Toronto. They were standing over Ru. Ru gasped loudly. Kanika screamed as she felt Ru's body get slammed against the taxi. Ru pounded her fist on the taxi's roof.

"Go! Go!" she yelled to the driver. But the driver saw Dragon pull back his jacket to reveal a gun. The taxi driver's hands stopped dead, like they were frozen to the wheel of the car.

"Move!" Kanika shouted at the driver from the back seat. Fear crippled every inch of her body.

Kanika could see through the windows of

the taxi, which was still not moving.

The balding man grabbed Ru and pulled her into the alley. Ru fought him all the way, but he overpowered her. Dragon and the blond ponytailed man stood with their eyes on the taxi driver.

"Get out!" Dragon growled at Kanika.

Kanika shook as she got out of the taxi. *This is going to be where I die*, she thought.

"Hey, who the hell is gonna pay me!?" the taxi driver yelled.

Dragon fired a shot in the air. The taxi squealed away from the curb. Kanika realized her bag was still in the back of the taxi. In it was all the money she had saved. She was right back to where she started. She was scared, embarrassed and out of hope. She was too afraid to look at Dragon.

"You want me to take care of this ho, Dragon?" the balding man called from the alley. Ru was still struggling to get free from his grip.

"Yeah, take care of her," Dragon ordered.

"Go ahead, do it! You crappy piece of shit!" Ru spit in the balding man's face. He fired a single shot at Ru. Kanika screamed as she watched Ru crumple to the ground.

The ponytailed man grabbed Kanika by the arm and pushed her down the sidewalk. "You're next!" he shouted.

Kanika looked up at the black sky. Her mother must have felt like this when she was killed in the hotel. She must have felt this horror, this panic. Kanika shook at the thought of her life ending the same way.

"Don't kill this one," Dragon said. "She needs to make up for my money she didn't make while she was faking sick!" Dragon squeezed Kanika's face so hard she thought her teeth would pop out.

"You let Ru get in your damn head," Dragon said to Kanika. "So listen to my words carefully. You can never get away from me. Ever. You don't know who I know, or what I know. And the next time you try to pull shit like this, you can say goodbye to your little brown face." Dragon pushed her back toward the ponytailed man.

"Mess her up, then put her to work," Dragon ordered. "I'd do it myself, but I'm too pissed off. If I put my hands on her right now, you'd be scraping *her* narrow Black ass off the street too. Take her to the hotel. I have a trick lined up and waiting."

The ponytailed man dragged Kanika around the corner to his car. Just before she stepped in, he punched her in the face. Kanika screamed. Then he jabbed her in the ribs. Kanika could feel the crack of her bones as they broke. While the man was pounding on her, all Kanika could think of was Ru's bloodied body lying in the alley. That image stuck in her head. It made her refuse to cry. Through her haze, she could see Dragon disappear into the alley where Ru's body was. Then Kanika passed out in the back seat of the car.

When they arrived at the hotel, the ponytailed man poured cold bottled water over Kanika's face. It jarred her awake. He yelled at her to clean herself up.

"And don't try anything stupid," he added. "Go to room one hundred and one. I'll be sitting here when you come out."

Kanika felt trapped. She couldn't call for help or get to the police. Her body ached as she got out of the car. She thought about what she had witnessed. *Does Ru have family? Will they ever know she has been killed in a lonely alley by a monster?* she wondered.

Kanika wiped the tears from her eyes and walked into the hotel. Maybe Panama was right. Maybe this hell *was* for life.

Chapter 18

Last Chance

"Bitches come and bitches go," Dragon said.

The girls kept asking about Ru, but no one ever got a real answer. Every day, Kanika would comb the papers. She hoped to find an article about a missing woman matching Ru's description. Or a news story about her body being found. But after some time, Kanika was quietly starting to give up hope.

"You girls know you're a dime a dozen." Dragon stood in the middle of the floor.

He was finally giving some answers about Ru. "Your girl, she went and got her ass shot off by a trick."

The girls gasped. Some of them screamed and cried out loud. Kanika shook with frustration at Dragon's lie.

But Dragon wasn't finished. He said, "So now I'm on the hunt for two more bitches. I need to replace Brittany and Ru. Both of them betrayed me and left me in a bad spot. You girls need to step up your game until I can get some new fire up in here."

Kanika watched him walk out. There was no remorse, no regret. He was cold and uncaring. He was a liar who cared about no one.

Kanika listened as the girls wept and shook their heads, saying, "poor Ru." If only they knew what really happened. Kanika hated Dragon. She couldn't stop the tears from pouring out. It was hard to keep the truth from the other girls. But she didn't dare tell the truth, not even to Panama. Instead, Kanika kept it all inside.

One night, Panama and Kanika had just returned home. They were hungrily munching on leftover chicken. Kanika decided to talk to Panama again about leaving.

"It's not as easy as that, Kanika," Panama replied.

"All we need to do is stick together. I know we can make it home."

"You didn't learn your lesson from the last time?"

"Are you happy here, Panama? Do you want this life?"

"Of course not!"

"So why won't you leave?"

"Do you think my parents will love me now? They won't ever have anything to do with me again once they find out what I've been doing here. Be real, Kanika. They can never find out about this."

"I like to think our families would understand."

"You think Aunt Becky will take you back? Not my family. Never. So stop talking about *going home*. Please. It's not home for me anymore."

Kanika didn't know what to say. She was on her own. She would have to try to make her way back to Nova Scotia alone.

Just then, Shay, a new girl, came rushing into the kitchen.

"You guys hear the news?" she panted.

"No," Panama answered.

"Dragon's mother was in the hospital for an operation. And she didn't survive the surgery."

"Really?" Kanika looked up. She wondered what that would mean for her.

"Dragon and Dawn are leaving in the morning for a whole week," Shay continued. "They're going for the funeral."

"Going where?" Kanika asked.

"Dragon is from British Columbia. That's where his mother died."

No Dragon for a whole week, Kanika thought. *And no Dawn.* She knew the other girls would stay loyal to them. They would be happy to show him how good they could be. They would keep bringing in big dollars in his absence to prove themselves. Even Panama was a part of the rivalry between the girls, all vying for Dragon's approval.

But Kanika knew she wasn't like Panama anymore. She wouldn't conform. She had no desire to please Dragon. She did what she had to do to stay alive.

Now, the chance to get out while Dragon was gone was too good to ignore.

"Poor Dragon. He must be crushed by this," Shay moaned.

"Dragon hated his mother, you fool." Dawn appeared in the doorway. "We're only going because he's named in the will.
He doesn't give a shit about the funeral."

Kanika shook her head in disgust.

"Oh, you're judging?" Dawn challenged her.

"No." Kanika looked down at her plate of chicken.

Later that night, the girls heard all the threats from Dragon about how they should be while he was away. When he left, they went to bed. Kanika knew Dragon's minions would be around to keep watch on them while he was gone. She had to be very careful every step of the way.

Kanika decided she would wait two days for the weekend to start. There were conventions going on, and it would be a busy weekend for the girls. They wouldn't figure out right away that Kanika was gone. They would think she was just out bringing in a lot of cash.

The next day was filled with anxiety. Kanika was alone with her thoughts of escaping. But she felt like every girl in the house could read her mind and see the plans in her head. She and Panama passed the day playing cards and gluing on fake nails.

"Hold your hand still, Kanika," Panama said as she tugged on Kanika's thumb. She took her slow time applying the tiny brush of glue to Kanika's narrow fingernail.

"Well, hurry up, then. It didn't take me this long to do yours."

"That's because I'm doing it right." Panama looked up at Kanika and sneered.

Kanika realized that if she managed to escape, she might never see her best friend again. Several times she was tempted to tell Panama what she was about to do. But she talked herself out of it each time.

"There!" Panama placed the fake nail across Kanika's thumb. Then she leaned back to admire her work. "Perfection," she boasted.

"Yeah, it looks good," agreed Kanika. "I guess it's true what they say about Asians and French manicures!"

Both girls laughed.

Kanika went over the plan in her head a million times, thinking about every possible way it could go. She wanted to be sure. This time she could not get caught.

It was nearly an hour before dawn. Kanika knew it was the only time she could slip out without being seen or questioned. She took one last look around her room. She planned to leave as she came — with nothing. She also planned to never come back.

Chapter 19

The Way Home

Kanika's fear was drowned by the deafening sound of her heart. It felt like it was beating out of her chest. She walked briskly through the empty darkness of Scarborough's back streets. She kept looking behind her as she walked, afraid she was being followed. Each time a car passed by, she would turn her body away from the road. She tried to be as invisible as she could. She was sweating beneath her clothes and across her forehead.

Her breathing was labored and heavy.
She prayed she would make it to a safe place
before Dragon found her.

Just when she felt she couldn't go any
further, Kanika came across a tiny hiding spot.
It was between the dumpster of an abandoned
apartment building and a high wooden fence.
On legs that could no longer carry her, she
stumbled across the overgrown shrubs and
slid behind the rusted green bin. The smell of
rotting food and strong urine burned her nose.
But that garbage bin was her protection for the
night. The thick, unkempt grass would be her
bed to lie on. The fence would keep unwanted
eyes from noticing her. Kanika curled up into a
ball and closed her eyes.

Sleep didn't last very long before the sun
burned Kanika's eyelids. It was early morning.
She breathed a sigh of relief that she had made
it through the night. But she knew there was
still danger. Kanika forced her tired body up
against the fence. She felt like she had been

thrown from a mountain and banged against the rocks the whole way down. She had to find strength to be able to make it to safety. She didn't have Panama to tell her she was making a dumb mistake. There was no Ru to help her get back to Nova Scotia. She was all alone.

The thought of that made her heart sink. She just wanted to be free to sleep in her own bed and hang out with her friends and fight with her aunt. Kanika felt sad that her life had come so far from normal. At first, the courage to take the first step away from the dumpster wouldn't come. Kanika's feet simply refused to move. Kanika had no plan. She was really scared.

A silent tear slid down her cheek and landed on her sweater. Kanika looked down at it. One tear gave way to another. Then another. Soon, she was bawling. She slid back down to the ground. Snot and tears caked her face. She wrapped her arms around her knees and drew them into her chin. No one back at the house cared where she was. No one from home would be looking for her after all this time.

If her mother was alive, Kanika was sure things would be different. Her mom would protect her from this life, from this kind of fear. "She wouldn't want this for me," Kanika said out loud. She wiped the mess of tears from her face. Hearing her own voice gave her enough strength to get moving.

Suddenly, Kanika heard a loud crash. She rose to her feet and peered around the garbage bin. Kanika rubbed her clouded eyes to see two men exit two cars that had collided. They began screaming at each other. Kanika remained frozen and unseen. Then one man swung a blow and knocked the other driver to the ground. The man who was hit got back to his feet and the two started fighting violently. People began to gather. Kanika knew she had to find a way out before she was spotted. And with her luck, it would be someone who knew Dragon.

With all the power she could muster, Kanika dipped around to the back of the building. There was a path leading into a wood. She sprinted the full length of the long brick building. Once she was safely on the path and hidden by trees, she leaned against one to catch her breath. In the distance she could hear sirens headed to the brawl in the street. She thought of running back. She could grab a police officer and scream for help.

But then she remembered that Dragon had friends in the police. Some of the clients were officers. She remembered the girls coming home crying after being harassed, arrested and released, or assaulted by police. The girls would talk about being treated like a criminal, when they were the ones in need of protection. Kanika decided not to take the chance. She darted off into the woods.

The creepy path led to a busy intersection. Traffic was steady but people on foot were scarce. Kanika tried to blend in with what little walking traffic there was. She felt weird in her skin. Weird in her clothes. She felt as if everyone was giving her a strange look. She felt like they knew where she had been, what she had done and what she had seen. She felt naked and exposed.

As she forced herself along the sidewalk, Kanika noticed a tall sign for Maystone Plaza. She headed for the breakfast place in the corner of the plaza. She didn't know what she would find there. But she hoped it might be a welcoming face that would help get her home.

Chapter 20

Trusting In Good

The diner was busy with eaters and rushing cashiers. It was filled with noisy chatter. Kanika slid into a booth with half-empty plates of food on the table. A woman with blonde hair in a ponytail skipped over to her with a smile.

"Hi, darling! Good day, isn't it? What can I get for you this morning?"

Kanika had no purse and no money. "I'll just have a water for now," she said.

"Sure thing! I'll grab your water and I'll be

back in a second to clear off that table."

The blonde waitress skipped away. Kanika waited until she was out of sight, then she hungrily attacked the food left behind by the previous customer. She rammed the food into her mouth, using the fork and her free hand.

Just as she was about to finish, she looked up from the plate. Her eyes landed right on a man sitting with his wife at the next table. Kanika was embarrassed. She looked over at the wife, who was trying not to make eye contact. Kanika pushed the plate away and wiped her face with a used napkin. Even she was grossed out by what she had done.

The server came over and plopped the glass of ice water on the table. Kanika grabbed it and gulped it back. The coldness trickling down the back of her throat felt good. The waitress stood waiting, her pen and pad in hand.

"Are we ready to order?" she finally said.

Kanika removed the glass from her lips. "Umm, I'm not hungry right now."

"Well you can't stay if you don't order." The server's tone changed. "Finish your water and beat it." She stuck her pad in her pocket and walked away.

The man got up from the next table and went to the counter to pay. From the corner of her eye, Kanika could see the wife staring at her. She kept glancing toward her husband to make sure he wasn't looking back.

"Here," the woman finally whispered. She held out a twenty-dollar bill to Kanika.

Kanika reached out and snatched the bill from the woman's hand.

"Buy yourself a real meal," the woman said.

"Thank you," Kanika said.

"Where you headed?"

"Nova Scotia."

"Alone?" The woman was still glancing up at the counter.

"Yeah."

"You got people there?"

"Yeah. I got nobody here."

"Ready, dear?" the man said as he came back to the table. He smiled.

The woman got up from her chair. Her husband helped her with her coat.

"I want to beat that crazy 401 traffic," he continued.

"Too late for that." His wife smiled.

The man started to walk toward the door.

"Wait." His wife called him back. "She's going to Nova Scotia," she said, looking at Kanika.

"So?" He shrugged.

"We can give her a ride."

"Are you crazy? We're not going that far."

"We're going to New Brunswick. That will get her most of the way."

Kanika stared at her hands while the couple argued. She was uncomfortable being the cause of their quarrel.

Finally the man let out a big sigh.

"You want a ride, honey?" the woman asked.

Kanika nodded. She tried not to show how close she was to crying.

"I am Ella and this is my husband, Tom. We're only going to Moncton. Maybe you can give your family a call to see if someone can meet you there?"

Those words stole the air from Kanika's throat. Picking up a phone and calling her aunt seemed like a dream to her. She was on her way home.

"Don't worry, everything will be just fine," said Ella. She smiled warmly. Kanika felt as if the woman could see all of her problems. "What's your name?" she asked.

"Kanika."

Kanika followed the couple out the door. She was exhausted. She wanted to stretch out across the back seat and sleep. But Ella talked their heads off for about three hours. Tom seemed used to it. Kanika finally dozed off. When she woke, Tom was pulling into a McDonald's.

"It's lunchtime," he announced. As they exited the car and stretched their legs, Tom whispered to Kanika. "Sorry, I should have warned you about how much she talks."

They both laughed.

Kanika hoped Tom knew how grateful she was for his and Ella's help. She thought about telling them how she ended up in Ontario. But she wasn't sure she could trust them. Even though she was driving hundreds of miles with them, they were still strangers. And Kanika was ashamed to expose her secrets.

As they chowed down on burgers and fries, Ella pulled out her cellphone. She handed it to Kanika.

"Here," she said. "Call your family."

Kanika's hand shook as the phone slid into her palm. She wondered if Aunt Becky would be mad. Maybe she thought Kanika had just run away. Maybe Aunt Becky would hang up as soon as she heard Kanika's voice on the line. How could she explain it to Tom and Ella?

Kanika slowly punched in the numbers. She held the phone close to her ear. She held her breath as the phone rang.

"Hello?" Aunt Becky's voice sounded weary.

"Aunt Becky?"

"Who is this?"

"It's me."

"Kanika? Is that you?"

"It's me." There was silence on the other end of the line. Was Aunt Becky about to hang up? Kanika waited. Still nothing. "Aunt Becky?"

"I'm here," she said at last. Kanika could tell she was crying.

"I'm coming home."

"Where have you been? I've been worried sick. I thought you were dead."

Kanika looked up to see Tom and Ella staring silently.

"I can't explain on the phone. Can you meet me in New Brunswick?"

"New Brunswick?"

"Yes. I'm in . . ." Kanika pulled the phone away from her ear. "Where are we?" she asked Tom.

"Quebec."

"I'm in Quebec right now," she said into the phone.

"Tell them we will be in Moncton in about ten hours," Ella jumped in.

Before hanging up, Aunt Becky asked Kanika why she had run away. Kanika ignored her question and brought the conversation back to the meeting spot. Aunt Becky pleaded with Kanika and made her promise they would have a long talk when Kanika was home. Kanika agreed. Anything to be back in her own room and bed again.

Chapter 21

The Rescue

Kanika sat up all night telling Aunt Becky about her ordeal. She told about Crystal, and how they were driven to Ontario by two thugs. She wasn't ready to talk about what happened with the men who paid to have sex with her. But she told about Panama and Dragon and Ru. She talked until her mouth was dry.

Aunt Becky grew more and more upset as Kanika told her about Dragon and the girls in the house.

"It's time for battle," Aunt Becky said.

Those were the last words Kanika heard before she dozed off to sleep.

The next day, Kanika woke to the smell of breakfast. She didn't want to leave her bed, but she was hungry. When she entered the kitchen, Aunt Becky motioned for her to sit down.

"I'm making your favourite," Aunt Becky said.

As they sat and ate, Aunt Becky spoke, "I never stopped looking for you, Kanika. I figured you took off because you were angry with me. Because I didn't like that boy you were hanging out with. I felt guilty. I thought I had been too hard on you."

"You *were* kinda hard on me, Aunt Becky."

"Only because I wanted to keep you on the right track."

"Guess that didn't work."

"This wasn't your fault, Kanika. But I can tell you, when I heard your voice on the other end of the line, I almost passed out. I called the rental place right away and guess what?"

"What?"

"The wheels of that rental car didn't touch the ground until I pulled into that train station in Moncton."

Kanika laughed.

"My heart kept beating fast. I kept saying, 'please don't let this be a joke.'"

Kanika replied, "I was so happy to see you standing there when I stepped out of Tom and Ella's car. It just didn't seem real."

"You are one brave cookie, Kanika Grace Adams." Aunt Becky leaned in and kissed Kanika's forehead.

"Now we have to get Panama out," said Kanika. She wouldn't feel right until Panama was home, too.

"Her parents and I are already on it. We spoke this morning."

"So what's the plan?"

"Well, this is where you come in. The police here and in Ontario will help find her and bring her back. But you are the key to making that happen. So, the police want to come and talk with you today. How do you feel about that?"

"Anything to help Panama. I owe her that."

Within a few weeks, Kanika found herself back in Ontario. This time, her aunt and Panama's parents were with her. The four of them were in room one hundred and fifteen of the Westside Hotel outside Scarborough. Crammed in with them was an Ontario Provincial Police detective and several officers. Kanika had told them how to find Panama. She had told them what they needed to know to help the other girls trapped under Dragon's cruel thumb. Kanika sat in a chair in the corner, trying to be invisible.

Being back in Ontario just a few short months after struggling to make her way home gave Kanika a really sick feeling. All she wanted was for Panama to get away from Dragon and be safe. Maybe Kanika and Panama could be close again. Panama's parents insisted that Kanika be there to help them bring Panama home. Kanika had told them that Panama's wish was to make Dragon happy and that she was afraid to leave him. That Panama had had the chance to escape with Kanika but refused. With Kanika close, they believed she could help convince Panama to come home.

The plan was to have a police officer act as a trick wanting a night with an Asian girl. Dawn set up the date for him to meet with Panama, not knowing that she was talking to an undercover. The detective set up shop in the room next to where Panama was to meet her trick.

Through the speaker, Kanika and Panama's parents could hear everything as it happened. Everyone was silent as Panama knocked on the hotel rooom door.

"Come in," said the undercover police officer.

"Hi." Panama's voice was soft as she stepped inside.

"Is your pimp outside waiting?"

"Yes."

"What . . . um . . . what can I get for two-hundred dollars?"

"One hour, whatever you want. But no anal." Kanika shot a look at Panama's parents. Her father seemed to be in shock by what his daughter was saying.

"Okay. Here's the money. I'm just putting it in your hand, okay?"

"Okay, move in on the perp downstairs. Now!" Kanika heard a detective shout through his walkie. "Carson and Craig, get in there, now! Take the father with you."

Kanika heard Panama scream as the officers barged into the room.

"Who the hell are you guys? What is this?" she yelled.

Kanika heard a scuffle.

"Get off of me, you assholes!" Panama screeched.

"Panama, they won't hurt you! It's me, Dad!"

Everything grew deathly silent in the hotel

room. Over the walkie, Kanika could tell that they had Dragon in handcuffs in the back of an unmarked car.

Kanika could barely believe it. Was Dragon finally going to jail? She wondered if the back of a car, or jail for that matter, could really contain him.

"Kanika?" Panama and her father entered the room with the two officers. Panama hugged her mother then ran to Kanika.

"You're alive! I thought Dragon caught you and got rid of you." Panama hugged Kanika tight.

Kanika suddenly felt a hint of resentment. Panama wouldn't escape with her. She left Kanika to do it all alone. Now Kanika helped Panama get rescued. As happy as she was to see her friend, Kanika wished they could have found their freedom together.

"I thought about you every day since you left, Kanika. You were so brave. I will never be as brave as you."

"Did Dragon come looking for me?"
Kanika asked.

"Yes. He sent people to Guysborough. But after a while he just stopped. I'm not sure why."

* * *

Back in Guysborough, Kanika spent a lot of time at Panama's house. Panama was having a hard time being back. She often called Kanika to come over to talk through what she was feeling. She told Kanika that she still didn't feel as if she could talk to her parents. They didn't know how to help her and couldn't figure it out. But Kanika understood Panama and Panama understood Kanika.

They sat around talking about what they went through in Ontario and how their friendship had changed. Each time, they felt like another brick had been chipped away from the walls they'd built around themselves.

Chapter 22

Normal

Kanika thought of her parents often. She
thought about Ru all the time. One day as
she made her way to Panama's house to visit,
a tear formed in the corner of her eye. She felt
she played a part in Ru's death. But she hadn't
been able to share that pain with anybody. By
the time Kanika got to Panama's house, she
was fully in tears. She told Panama everything
about Ru's death. She told her about what she
had found out about her parents.

"I've been thinking about what you said," Panama told her. "You know, about wanting to move to the city?"

"Yeah," Kanika replied.

"Were you serious? I mean . . . do you want to leave Guysborough?"

"Oh, really, really badly."

"Let's do it!"

"Okay."

The girls hugged as Kanika headed out the door to go home. It was getting close to suppertime. Kanika was in the mood for the pork chops she'd seen thawing on the counter earlier in the day. She walked in to the smell of pork cooked in mushroom sauce with garlic mashed potatoes.

Aunt Becky watched Kanika eat.

"Please stop staring," Kanika finally said.

"I'm sorry, Kanika. I'm still worried about you. You won't really talk about what happened. I've been telling you that I'm here for you. But you won't let me help."

"Here we go again."

"I mean, they said I should give you time. But this has been too much time."

"Aunt Becky, I'm moving out," Kanika announced.

"What? Where did that come from?"

"Panama and I have been planning it a while. It's time for us to get out of Guysborough."

"Leave Guysborough? Kanika, are you sure you're ready for that? You're only sixteen. Where do you plan to go?"

"Halifax. There's nothing here for us. It's like a trap. We want to get an apartment in the city, find jobs and get some freedom."

"I give you lots of freedom."

"Yes, for a ten-year-old. I'm not a kid anymore, Aunt Becky. I stopped being a kid when I stepped into that car with Danny."

Kanika couldn't face the confusion in Aunt Becky's face. She knew she was letting her aunt down. But her aunt had let her down as well.

"I saw the article," Kanika said.

"What article?"

"My mother was a sex worker. My dad was her pimp."

"Oh, Kanika. I'm so sorry about that."

"Why didn't you just tell me? I had to read about it in that article in the garage."

"I was trying to protect you. Waiting for the right time."

"But I had so many questions. You had the answers."

"I didn't know how to tell you. I was only thinking of you."

Kanika knew in her heart that her aunt wanted the best for her. Aunt Becky had proved that when she hopped in a car and drove all the way to Moncton to pick her up. And when she helped to bring Panama home.

"I didn't want you to end up like her," Aunt Becky explained. "Your mother got caught up. Just like you. I did everything to help her get out, but she didn't want to come

179

home. She was my little sister and I tried to protect her. But she was in love with Fred and no one could tell her anything."

"My mom wasn't forced into it?"

"No. That's how they made their money."

"But why did she want to do that? And why did he let her?"

"Your mother fell in love with a pimp. That life was all he knew and she didn't care. I think she loved the thrill of the game."

Kanika thought of Ru. She thought she finally understood her mom and Aunt Becky.

"Please let it go, Aunt Becky. Don't judge my mother anymore. She wasn't any less of a good woman than you are. She had a heart and feelings."

Kanika could tell that Aunt Becky was shocked. But then she sighed. "You are right, Kanika. And I think that was my biggest mistake. Your mother was truly a beautiful person with a good heart. But all I could see was how she made her living."

"Everybody judges."

"That's why I don't want you to go, Kanika. I lost you once. And I don't want anything to happen to you again. This is your home and you belong here."

"Aunt Becky, Panama and I don't belong here anymore. You can pretend it's not true if you want to. But you can see it. People stare at us. We know they talk about us all the time. I thought it would stop at some point. But we've been back a long while and nothing has changed. I'm tired of feeling dirty. I'm tired of stupid questions from old women from the church who see me at the store. They treat me like I'm the devil."

"You have to ignore them."

"Even if I ignore them, how do I get the nightmares out of my head? This is where I was taken from. I feel like any day Dragon will show up and drag me back to Ontario. Do you know how scary that feels?"

"Kanika, Dragon won't be coming back to Guysborough for you."

"You don't know that."

Aunt Becky began to tear up again. She dropped her fork onto the plate and placed her half-eaten food on the counter before she left the kitchen. Kanika heard her aunt's bedroom door slam.

Kanika finished her supper and left the house. A walk along the lonely gravel road to Panama's house was just what she needed.

She was glad that she and Becky had finally talked about her parents. But she didn't think Aunt Becky would ever be okay with Kanika wanting to leave Guysborough.

Panama was stretched out on her bed when Kanika walked in. Kanika kicked off her shoes and stretched out on the bed beside her friend.

"Aunt Becky problems again?"

"Yeah," Kanika sighed.

"At least she *wants* to be on your back about it. My parents are the opposite. My mother is scared to death to ask me anything about Ontario. Yesterday in the car, Dad started to ask me something about Dragon. My mom punched him in the arm."

"That's crazy." Kanika chuckled. "Aunt Becky said my mother *wanted* to be a sex worker for my dad."

"Like Ru."

"Yeah, like Ru."

"Kanika?"

"Yes?"

"Are we normal?"

Kanika thought about the girls they were before this all happened. Kanika rebelling against her Aunt Becky's rules. Panama trusting everyone to tell the truth and do the right thing. There had been no place in their lives for pimps and sex work and terror. They had been fifteen years old and innocent. She knew the answer to her friend's question.

"Normal, Panama? Not anymore."

Acknowledgements

I wish to thank all of those first voices, who have lived through similar situations and found the courage to share those experiences with me. To those who gave their authentic input and constructive feedback, the good and not-so-good, I am grateful to you. And to those working the front lines on the battlefield, fighting injustice every day, I thank you for reminding me that this subject matters. And lastly a huge thank you goes out to my family — my *ride or die* supporters no matter what.